The Dancing Dolls

By Trevor William Poate

Published with CompletelyNovel.com
Unit A3, Masterlord Industrial Estate
Leiston, Suffolk
IP16 4JD

www.completelynovel.com

ISBN: 978-1-849140-85-0

The Dancing Dolls

First published in 2011 with CompletelyNovel.com
Copyright © **Trevor William Poate 2011**

If you would like more information about this title, the author, or would like to write a review of this book please visit www.completelynovel.com

Trevor William Poate

Acknowledgements

I would like to thank Martin McCaffrey, John Staite, Jon Scott and David Wright for their unstinting reading abilities and encouragement.

Trevor William Poate

Trevor William Poate

The Dancing Dolls

Trevor William Poate

Part One

A Complex Situation

Trevor William Poate

The Dancing Dolls

Trevor William Poate

Chapter 1

Community Day

I'd never seen any plants growing wild, or anything wild for that matter. So, I was surprised when there was a small growth in the ground a few metres away from our Multiplex. I couldn't investigate it for obvious reasons, but I was intrigued. It was out of place in the dark yellow earth, scorched by the relentless sun shining through the clear, light blue, sky. The sky was always clear and light blue. I'd been told there had been clouds at one time; fluffy white things, floating high up, but I'd never seen any, and wasn't sure they had ever really existed. But then again, I had never seen a plant with my own eyes before now.

'Calista. Come and look at this,' I called across the room.

She joined me, her shoulder length light brown hair bouncing as she crossed the room. She looked through the thick glass window, at where I was pointing.

'What is it Callum?'

'I think it's a plant, but I'm not sure.'

'Where do you think it came from?'

'I don't know.'

We both stood, silently watching the small green object sway in the breeze. We'd never felt a breeze, because we weren't allowed outside.

'Should we report it?' she said, putting her nose up to the glass.

'I'll ask Bertrum when we see him...'

The Observation room was the only part of our Multiplex not underground. It was circular, and made from six centimetre thick white plastic, which was hermetically sealed to ensure the toxic gasses didn't infiltrate from outside. It had eight glass windows, allowing us to view the landscape in all directions and a door to the outside. We'd never opened it, but it was there in case we needed to evacuate, or if it ever became safe to leave.

The four-metre diameter room held all the outside measuring instruments needed to record the information for the Centre. We used the equipment to make our daily observations. What the Centre did with them was a mystery, but if we failed to send them we got into trouble, despite them being almost the same every day. The equipment recorded the wind speed and it's intensity, the outside temperature at noon and midnight, and the atmospheric gas measurements. At one time the data was sent automatically, but the equipment had begun failing years before, like many things. We were also supposed to report anything unusual we saw, such as changes to the landscape. The plant was unusual.

'...he'll know what to do,' I said.

'Alright,' she said, quietly.

Trevor William Poate

We finished collecting the data and made our way to the airlock. It was our last line of defence if the Observation room leaked. It sealed the room from the rest of the Multiplex below ground. Our first daily task was over. Before leaving I switched off the E glass, and it returned to it's opaque condition. The glass contained a filament which, when an electric current was passed through, changed it from opaque to clear. It was just after dawn and the sky was changing colour from an orangey pink to it's daytime light blue as the sun slowly rose in the sky.

We entered the airlock, sealed the door, refreshed the air, and opened the door into the lift, which would take us down thirty-five metres to our living and working areas. The almost silent lift took only a minute to reach the bottom, where the door opened into a circular atrium, which had eight corridors leading from it.

The Multiplex was powered by batteries, charged from photoelectric power cells located on the roof of the Observation room. My next task was to check they were working to capacity.

'I'll check the power readings,' I said, as we left the lift.

'Ok. I'm going to the scrubbers to check the air readings. I'll see you in the Work room,' Calista replied.

Each room in the Multiplex was connected to the atrium by a three-metre diameter tube, or corridor. Everything was circular for safety, and built from the same, ten centimetres thick, white plastic. Corner joints were more likely to fail, and leak. Nearly everything was made from plastic because it didn't biodegrade in the toxic earth and rock surrounding the Multiplex. I made my way along the tube leading to the Power room and took the readings from the instruments monitoring the batteries and power cells. They were well within the safe limits laid down by the Centre.

Calista went to the Air-conditioning room containing the scrubbers. It was where our breathable air was produced. Every room in the Multiplex had a ventilation system, connected by pipes to the scrubbers. Harmful gasses were removed from the air, which was then recycled for our use. Every six months the filters were replaced. We were getting close to needing replacements, so it was important to monitor their efficiency. We kept replacements in the Multiplex, and sent used ones back to the Centre for cleaning.

My final task was to check the water pressure. Water was piped from the Centre where it was produced from recycled wastewater. Water pressure was very important to us. A significant drop might mean a leak; something we couldn't afford. We were given a daily allowance, which was just enough to meet our needs. Any leak might cause a shortage, or even mean contamination from the surrounding earth, which was potentially fatal. We also monitored the quality of the water. It contained minerals essential for our survival. The humidity of the Multiplex was also monitored. It was important to retain some moisture in the air, but because the Multiplex was sealed, the level had to be kept as low as possible to avoid condensation forming.

Most of our support systems had been developed from space technology, nearly sixty years before. Occasionally they were upgraded, but the essential equipment was very old and needed close attention, which was why we took the readings. Or so the Officers in the Centre told us.

During our period of education, we had learned that ten Complexes had been built around the world. Each Complex comprised fourteen hundred Multiplexes, attached to a Centre, housing two thousand eight hundred adults and eight hundred children. Each Complex was populated by one racial group; European, Oriental, Asian, Arab, North American, Central American and Caribbean, South American, Australasian and Pacific, North and West African and, Southern and Central African.

The Officers only had twelve years notice to design and build the Complexes. We were the living results of the selection process to decide who would be allocated a place in one of them. None of the original people were still alive, and we were the third generation born and bred there. The Complexes were built in the most isolated parts of the planet, to avoid the possibility of contamination. We lived in the European Complex, situated in the Sahara Desert.

I met Calista in the Work room where she was waiting for me.

'The filters will need changing next week,' she

said, as I entered.

'I'll advise the Centre.'

'Is everything else alright?'

'Yes. The toxin levels are down again.'

'Do you think that has anything to do with the plant?'

'I don't know.'

She looked at me, possibly for guidance, but I didn't know any more than she did.

'Ok. I'll see to breakfast.' She turned away towards the door and, pausing, said. 'We should try and find out.'

'Yes, I'll ask Bertrum.'

She'd left me the air readings, and as she made her way to the Feeding room I started entering the data into the computer. Everything was controlled by the computer systems, except the data readings. We were linked to the Centre by a high speed fibre optic cable, and each Complex was connected to the other Complexes by a satellite link. Before 'The Collapse' almost everyone in the World was connected in a similar way at work and at home. After fifteen minutes, I joined her.

Food was purely for nourishment. It was provided by the Centre, in packs produced specifically for each of us. The Centre monitored our physical condition once a week, and adjusted our food packs according to the results. All our dietary requirements were catered for. The packs consisted of a glutinous paste which, when opened, reconstituted itself into a meal when it was mixed with water, and heated. We ate it with a spoon. Neither of us had ever tasted naturally grown food, so we were quite happy with the paste. We collected the packs from the Centre once a week, on our Community Day, after the Centre had prepared them for us. Our Community Day was that day. We would have our physical checks and collect our food packs before returning.

We knew that any disease could spread very quickly, and accepted the sterile conditions we lived in for our own safety. We had been told the Central American and Caribbean Complex had been compromised twenty years before, when someone had opened a door to the outside. Occasionally people did get sick, and were quarantined immediately. They were usually never seen again, and no one asked what happened to them. We didn't want to know. The Officers took care of them.

The Officers managed the Complex. They were graded A. B grade people were the Medical, Nutritional and Scientific groups. C grade people were the Educational, Production and Technical groups, and D grade people were the Maintenance, Cleaning and Security groups. Calista and I were grade C. The Multiplexes we lived in were of a different quality for each grade. I'd never been to a Multiplex other than a grade C, so didn't know what the differences were.

Calista was a junior educator, and I was a technician. Five days a week she taught children from the community, using holographic interaction, while I ran the computer systems. Every child, regardless of grade, received the same junior education, after which their work training was geared to their grade and taught by senior educators. One day a week was allocated to our Community Day, and the last day was our rest day.

Each Multiplex had a Work room. In our case, the room was used as a classroom. In other cases people worked machines from them, using the computer systems. The computer systems were complicated. I had spent four years learning how to use and maintain them. Calista had spent a similar length of time training as a junior educator of three to fourteen year olds, the age when children started training for work.

Almost the only choice we had in life was our coupling. We were obliged to find a suitable partner as soon as we completed our work training. Prior to that we lived with our parents. I had known Calista from infancy. We had played together on our Community Day meetings, the only time we ever met other people directly, and had applied to be coupled as soon as we were old enough; eighteen years of age. The rules were simple. We would be allowed to couple as long as we had compatible work skills and the same grade. We met the criteria, and after psychological and physical tests for personal compatibility, the Officers approved our coupling.

We didn't yet have any children, but had applied for permission to have one, and were eagerly waiting to hear the outcome of our application, later that day. It wasn't a formality. Not every couple was given approval to parent. New children had to be approved by the

Officers. No natural conceptions were allowed, and sex was only for pleasure. All males were sterilised one year after puberty. Their sperm was graded according to their heritage, and stored for later use. Similarly, women were sterilised after sufficient eggs had been taken and stored, usually two years after puberty. If we were approved to have a child we wouldn't know who the donors were. The sperm and egg were unlikely to be ours. We were told this was to ensure genetic improvements. With such a small population, the Officers were wary of genetic deformities creeping into the gene pool. All we knew was, the donors would be from the same grade as us.

A child would only be approved when someone died within our grade. We were told this was to maintain the population level in each Complex, which was important if the community was to survive. The Officers determined the gender of the child, otherwise we had all the approved genetic choices to make.

'Do you think we'll get approval today?' I asked, as I sat down opposite her at the feeding table.

'I hope so,' she said, looking up at me.

We continued to eat our breakfast in silence. The decision whether we could have a child was one of the most important in our lives. If we were given approval we would have to wait our turn, and not knowing was weighing on our minds.

We both finished eating, and I put the dishes into the cleaner, which doubled as a waste disposal unit. The small amount of waste was macerated, and sent by refuse pipes back to the Centre for recycling. Nothing came into the Complex from outside. The Centre had an enormous storage facility, which had been filled when it was built with enough non recyclable items to keep us alive for seventy five years, the amount of time the scientists thought it would take for the toxins outside to subside to safe levels. The toxin levels were still too high, and there was always pressure on us to conserve our resources as much as possible. The small amount of non-recyclable waste was ejected outside, after being treated with chemicals.

'The shuttle will be here soon,' I said, as I finished loading the cleaner. 'We'd better get ready.'

The shuttle was due at eight o'clock. Each Multiplex had a Transport room where the shuttle stopped to collect us. The shuttles travelled in tunnels connected to the Centre. If we missed ours when it arrived to collect us, we would be in serious trouble. It was only scheduled to stop at our Multiplex on our Community Day, to collect us in the morning, and return us in the evening. If we needed it at any other time, we had to contact the Centre and explain why.

The maintenance and cleaning people also used it. They visited our Multiplex each week when we were at the Centre. They repaired any damage we had reported, then cleaned and sterilised it. They also brought our weekly supply of clothes and took away our used ones. Our airspec clothes were a simple one-piece garment made from blue synthetic cloth, which we changed every day for clean ones. Each grade had a different coloured suit. Orange for grade A, Yellow for grade B, and green for grade D.

The shuttle levitated over a steel track using linear motors. This meant it was almost silent and maintenance free. It was built from the same white plastic used for our Multiplexes, without any windows. The shuttle we used on our Community Day stopped at thirty Multiplexes. There were fifteen stops after ours, and we would reach the Centre about an hour later. Other shuttles collected people from another two hundred Multiplexes, bringing a total of six hundred adults and their children together, on each of the six Community Days held each week. Each Community Day was limited to only one grade, which meant we rarely interacted with anyone from another grade.

'Callum,' Calista said, 'do you think it's now safe outside?'

'I don't know. The Scientists will tell us when it is.'

'But, if plants are growing, surely the toxin levels must be very low.'

'Perhaps, but we don't know what a safe level is. We can ask some of the others if they know.'

'Be careful. We don't want to get into any trouble.'

'I will, don't worry. We should go now.'

We left the Feeding room, made our way to the atrium and along the corridor to the Transport room. It was also protected by an air lock, which led to a small platform where we would wait for the shuttle. We entered the airlock, sealed the door behind us, and opened the door leading to the platform. When the shuttle arrived, the door allowing us to enter it would open automatically.

We were a few minutes early, and waited in silence. We would know where the shuttle was by the series of lights above the door. A red light told us the tunnel was empty. It turned to yellow when the shuttle was due, and green just before the door opened. It was still red when Calista spoke.

'Do you want a girl or a boy?'

'I don't mind,' I said. 'They'll tell us what we can have, if we get approved.'

'I want a girl first,' she said.

I didn't reply. Any child was fine by me. If we were allowed a second child later on, it would be the other gender, so we would have one of each anyway. Most couples were approved to have two children.

The light above the door changed to yellow. We both looked at it, waiting for the green light telling us the shuttle had arrived. A few seconds later it changed to green and the door slid open. We entered and took our allocated seats. The compartment held fifty people, but was only half full. We knew everyone sitting around us and nodded to them as we sat down. The couple sitting opposite us, Bertrum and Sally, smiled. Their year-old son, John, was next to them in a cradle, sleeping.

'It's your big day,' Sally said.

'Yes,' Calista replied nervously, 'I hope so.'

'I'm sure you'll be approved. Don't worry,' Bertrum said, smiling at her.

I looked at Calista. She badly wanted a child, and I could tell she was nervous. I wanted a child as well, but it was different for men. The Scientists and Doctors had been trying unsuccessfully for years to produce children without having to impregnate women, but they were still needed to carry the child for nine months. Nature always had the last say.

Sally worked in production. Her Work room was connected to the Centre's food production system. She controlled some of the machinery which produced our food. Bertrum, like me, was a technician running the equipment Sally used. There were more technicians than any other grade, because of the complexity of the computer systems, but his speciality was different from mine, because of Calista's need for holographic connectivity in her teaching work. Bertram's skills were tailored to managing the array of computers Sally used to manufacture, and ensure the quality of, our food. Each person's rations were unique to them, making her work very important, and very complicated.

I was wondering when I should ask Bertrum about the plant, when he leant over towards me and quietly said. 'Have you noticed anything unusual outside recently?'

I paused for a moment. 'Such as?' I asked, glancing at Calista.

He turned to Sally, as though he needed her approval to continue. 'Anything that wasn't there before,' he said, glancing around the shuttle.

'Have you?' I asked, reluctant to admit anything until I knew what he had to say.

'Yes. We have.'

'What?'

'We think it's a plant.'

'So have we,' Calista said, looking at me.

Karl, who was sitting behind us with his partner, Monica, must have overheard our conversation, because he turned round and said. 'We have too. We first saw one last week.' They had recently coupled, and didn't have any children either.

'What do you think it means?' I asked him.

'I don't know. Monica thinks the toxins may have dropped to safe levels. It may be safe to go outside.'

'Have you reported it to the Centre?'

'Not yet. Have you?'

'No we haven't. We only saw it for the first time this morning. We thought we'd ask Bertrum if he'd seen anything.'

We were all quiet for a few moments. We knew we should have reported the plants, and knew we could get into trouble for not doing so.

'Will you tell the Officers today?' Calista said to Bertrum.

'I want to talk to some other people first. If there are lots of plants we should all ask what the situation is.'

'Do you think they will tell us?' I said.

'Why not?'

Trevor William Poate

'I don't know. But I don't think they tell us everything.'

'We have to go to the Maternity Centre after our medical check. We could meet you in the Community room afterwards. If you can find out anything from the others by then, we could ask the Officers, as a group, at our briefing session,' Calista said.

Bertrum looked at Karl, and said. 'Will you help ask the others?'

'Yes we will,' he said, looking at Monica, who nodded agreement.

The shuttle came to a stop. One of the other compartments was open for people to enter. We sat in silence until it moved again.

'If it is safe, what will happen?' Monica said.

The rest of us looked at each other. None of us knew.

'The Officers will know,' I said.

Chapter 2

The Centre

*W*e made our way, along with the others, to the Medical Centre. The routine medical check only took a few minutes. A pinprick of blood was taken from each of us, analysed during the day, and the results passed to the Nutritional Centre by computer. The Nutritional Centre used the results to adjust our food packs. It involved adjusting the nutrients each of us needed to keep our body chemicals in balance. If anything outside of normal levels was detected, we would be told the following week, and further tests would be made. Anything serious may mean we didn't return to our Multiplex that day. We would be retained in the Medical Centre for corrective medication until the doctors were satisfied we were back to normal. If it was serious we might be quarantined, and the Officers would look after us.

The Medical Centre was located on level seven. It was busy as we queued waiting our turn. Six hundred people needed to be processed within an hour and a half. When it came to our turn we simply passed through a scanner which read the microchip embedded in our heads, identifying each of us. The microchip allowed the officers to track each of us anywhere in the Complex. We then inserted a finger into a hole, and waited, while it took the sample of blood for testing. If there had been a problem the week before, a message would come up telling us to report to a diagnostic booth where a doctor would give us a further examination. Calista and I were both clear and, when we'd finished, made our way to the Maternity Centre on the floor above.

Our appointment was scheduled for ten o'clock. We were both nervous about the outcome when we made our way to the consulting room. The doctor was waiting for us, and he smiled as we sat down next to his workstation.

'Congratulations to you both. We have completed the review of your application, checked your physical condition for child bearing, Calista, and you have approval to parent a girl.'

Calista smiled at me, leant over, and put her hand in mine. She was almost in tears with happiness.

'The next stage is to complete the chromosome assignments,' the doctor continued. 'As you know you have twenty two chromosomes, not including the sex chromosome, made up of nearly three billion genes. You have fifteen sets of choices to make. The rest are made by us, for the benefit of the child. I'll explain each choice to you, and then you should enter your choices into the computer system in your Multiplex. during the week. The choices are straightforward, but they are limited by the sperm and egg which have been allocated to you. All the donor sperms and eggs have been adjusted to remove the risk of any congenital diseases, so you don't need to worry about that. Wherever possible we match your personal genes to those of the donors. We don't want, for example, to give you a baby which will have no resemblance to yourselves, such as black skin, when you are both white. But of course, that can't happen in this Complex. For example, in your case you have the choice of blue or green eyes, black or brown straight or wavy hair, etcetera. I'll go through them all with you now, but there is an instruction pack available on computer site 48, which you have been given access to this morning, along with the data entry screen for you to select your choices. I'll give you the access code before you leave.'

'Can we ask questions if we need to?' Calista asked, looking at the form he had given her.

'Yes. There is a link to one of our advisors on the site.'

'When will I be impregnated?'

'Once we receive your selections, we will process them, make sure they are correct, adjust the genes of the sperm and egg, and then we will be ready to start. It takes eight weeks. During your Community Days between next week and your impregnation you will attend some classes explaining the whole process, what will happen to your body during the pregnancy and what to do if you have any problems. You will also attend the classes, Callum. The impregnation requires you both to stay here for the first week, after which you can go back to your Multiplex. We will, of course, monitor your condition each week on your

Community Day.'

'How long will I be able to work?'

'Assuming everything goes to plan, you will work up to a week before inducement. We induce at thirty nine weeks if you haven't gone into labour naturally. After the birth you will stay here for a week while we make checks on the baby's health and it's gene profile. We also complete the feeding program for the baby. As you know, we don't allow breast feeding. After that you can go back to your Multiplex and should be back at work again in another week. During the periods Calista is here, we will arrange for you, Callum, to complete some additional training. This allows you to see each other during these crucial periods.'

The doctor spent the next forty five minutes explaining all the choices we had to make, and answering our questions. It was daunting having to decide so much of a new person's life before they were even conceived.

The hour had passed very quickly. We were both excited when we left the Maternity Centre and made our way up three floors to the Community room. There was so much information and so many choices to make.

We'd been told we could discuss the whole process with our friends and parents. Both our parents had died the year before, so we decided to speak with Bertrum and Sally. They had been through the process when they had John, and we hoped they would help us make some of our choices. They were waiting for us in one of the lounge areas allocated to conversation, when we entered the Community room.

The Community room took up the whole of the third floor. Like every other part of the Centre, it was under surveillance by the Officers using cameras. It was split into various areas by soundproof partitions. There were lounge areas, holographic cinemas, a crèche, a fitness centre, and life skill areas where we could get instruction on almost anything we had an interest in. There was also an electronic library, where we could download books and music selected from the seventeen million available, onto our personal workbooks. Each of us had a workbook, which was a small handheld computer we could use for whatever purpose we wished. Some people used it for a diary, some to listen to music, and some to read books.

'How did you get on?' Sally asked, as we sat down next to her.

'We've been approved to parent a girl,' Calista replied excitedly.

'Congratulations.'

'The doctor said I would be impregnated in eight weeks.'

'That's very quick. I had to wait four months.'

'He explained about the choices we have. We are hoping you might advise us on some of them. How did you decide?'

'It took us ages. Some are quite straightforward, such as the physical ones, but the intellectual ones were difficult. We thought it would be best if we gave John interests similar to ours, because we could help him develop more easily.'

'What did you give him?'

'As you know, I play oboe in one of the orchestras, so we gave him an interest in music. Bertrum likes studying geography, so we gave him an interest in that as well. For our third choice we gave him an interest in science.'

Sally played in an orchestra on her rest day. She used the holographic connection in their Multiplex. This enabled her to play with others interested in music, without ever meeting any of them.

'We'll need to give that some thought,' I said.

'Yes, we will,' Calista replied, smiling at me and squeezing my hand.

'Have you asked anyone else about the plants?' I said.

Bertrum glanced at Sally. 'We tried, but most people wouldn't talk to us,' he said. 'One or two did, but they sounded scared, and advised us to keep quiet.'

'Why?' I said, surprised at the secrecy.

'Apparently someone asked the Officers, two weeks ago, about the atmosphere outside, and was told to report to one of the consulting rooms on level two, with his partner. No one has seen them since. The rumour is they have been put into quarantine.'

'What's wrong with them?' Calista said.

'We don't know, but not many people return from

there,' Sally replied.

'What should we do?'

'Keep quiet, if you want your baby.'

I looked at Calista, and said. 'But, if it is safe outside, why are we not being told?'

'We don't know,' Bertrum replied, in a whisper.

'Do you know if anyone has reported the plants?'

'Keep your voice down,' Sally said, looking around to see if anyone was listening. 'Some people have.'

I glanced around and, lowering my voice, said. 'What were they told?'

'They weren't told anything, but when they took the readings in their Observation room the next morning, the plants had gone.'

'Gone?'

'Apparently.'

'But that means someone must have been outside and removed them,' Calista said.

'Probably.'

'Have your toxin readings been falling?'

'Yes, they have.'

'So have ours. Do you know what a safe reading is?'

'No. We've never been told.'

'Neither have we.'

'We could ask at the briefing session,' I suggested.

'I don't know about that. It would need more than just us to ask, otherwise we'd probably get into trouble,' Bertrum replied.

'What sort of trouble?'

'Quarantine?'

'But we're not ill!'

'I don't think that matters. I think the Officers use the quarantine process to remove anyone causing trouble.'

'But we're not causing trouble. All we want to know is what is happening outside.'

'I don't think they want us to know.'

'Sally. When did your parents die?' Calista asked.

'Soon after Bertrum and I coupled. Why?'

'Are your parents alive, Bertrum?'

'No. They died around the same time.'

'Our parents also died soon after we coupled. Do you know any couples with parents still alive?'

Sally and Bertrum looked at each other for a moment, before Bertrum said. 'No, I don't think we do.'

'Don't you think that's strange?'

'Why should it be?'

'Well, surely some parents survive their children's coupling.'

'I don't know. I've never really thought about it,' Sally said.

'It just seems strange that, apart from a few of the Officers, I've never seen anyone older than about forty five or fifty. Just look around.'

We all glanced around the room. There was nobody older than about forty five.

'I've wondered about that for a while. It seems to me that once we stop parenting, at about that age, we die.

We were just told our parents had died. We never saw them again once we'd coupled,' Calista said. 'It seems strange that we couple, parent children, then mysteriously die, all at roughly the same age. Before The Collapse people lived for eighty or ninety years, but not now…'

'When did you start thinking about that?' I asked, interrupting her.

'A while ago.'

'You never said anything to me.'

'I know. I thought at first I was imagining it, but when I started looking around I noticed there were no old people, except some of the Officers.'

'So you think they are being killed off.'

'I don't know, but it does seem odd.'

'But that would be murder,' Sally said, clearly shocked at the idea.

'Or euthanasia.'

'So why don't the Officers die?'

'I don't know, but think about it. When the Complexes were built, only healthy fertile people in their twenties were accepted. They then had children which, when they coupled, became parents and their parents died. That has kept the population stable ever since. The first people had children naturally, but every generation since has been conceived artificially, and controlled by the Officers.'

'But the Officers have told us that we are conceived that way to ensure our survival,' I said.

'Exactly. That's what we've been told, but we only

know what they tell us.'

'What do you mean?'

'Well, how do we really know it's unsafe outside?'

'The Collapse made it unsafe.'

'Did it? We only know that because the Officers have told us it's unsafe.'

'But everything outside of the Complexes became toxic, and died.'

'Did it? We've all seen the plants,' she said looking at each of us. 'All the Complexes were built in arid regions, far away from the old populations. This one is in the Sahara Desert. Nothing lived here anyway. We don't really know if anyone survived elsewhere or not. We don't really even know if there are any other Complexes.'

'Why has no one thought of this before?' Sally said.

'Perhaps they have. Or maybe there have never been plants before, so no one asked any questions.'

'It all sounds like science fiction to me,' I said, looking at the large clock on the wall. 'We should go. It's time for our briefing session.'

The weekly briefings took place on the fourth level, in a lecture room holding two hundred of us at a time. There were three briefings held during each Community Day. Only the adults attended, while the older children looked after the younger ones in the crèches, with help from nursery attendants. The sessions lasted an hour, and were usually conducted by four Officers. During them we were told about any new regulations, news relating to other Complexes, and appointments to the Officer's Council, which managed the Complex. Occasionally we were told about any changes to our water or food rations, and the status of the atmosphere outside, which never seemed to change favourably. Questions were not encouraged.

The four of us were silent as we made our way to the staircase leading to the floor below. People were hurrying up and down the stairs, some leaving the previous briefing, others going to ours. There seemed to be some excitement in the chatter of those leaving the first one. I couldn't make out what was being said, as we hurried along, but I could tell something important had been announced.

The room was nearly full as we entered through the double doors, and found four seats next to each other near the back. Within a few minutes the room was full, and the presiding Officer called for quiet.

'Good morning everyone,' he said. 'I will go through a few routine items first, and then Robina from the Science group will address you.'

It was rare for anyone other than an Officer to address us. There was a murmur around the room, which soon died down as the Officer started speaking again. He told us the latest toxin results, advised us of some changes to the Community Day schedules and, rather ominously, reminded us it was our duty to advise the Centre of anything new we saw outside our Observation rooms. He then turned to Robina and invited her to address us. She stood up and slowly looked around the room. She was wearing a yellow airspec suit, and I guessed she was about forty years old.

'Some of you have reported plants in the vicinity of your Multiplexes. We are aware there are questions being asked amongst you about their significance. Over the last few weeks we have taken samples of these plants, and conducted full analyses of their structure, DNA, and chemical composition, under strict quarantine conditions. The results of our work indicate these plants are highly toxic to humans and are a mutation of a plant called a cactus, which lived in desert regions prior to The Collapse. Our analyses of the atmosphere outside the Complex confirms it is still unsafe for us to leave.'

She paused, to allow some murmurings among us to die down, before continuing.

'It is likely that more mutant plants will be observed over the coming weeks and months. It is therefore very important that you report any sightings as soon as you see them, so that we can take samples for further analyses. We are concerned that these plants will propagate further toxins in the atmosphere, and are working as quickly as we can to develop a method of killing them before they mature and seed. At this stage we don't know where they came from, but have been in touch with the other Complexes to find out if they have similar plants in their vicinities. As far as we know, this Complex is the only one affected. We will keep you informed of our progress each week. Thank you.'

She sat down amid a rising level of noise as we started talking amongst ourselves. Before the presiding Officer could continue the meeting, a man near the front stood up and asked Robina what would happen if the Science group couldn't find a way of killing the plants. The room returned to silence.

She remained sitting, glanced at the presiding Officer who nodded to her, and then said. 'At this time we don't know.'

'Could the plants help remove the toxins outside, and clean the atmosphere enough for us to leave here?' the man continued.

'That is unlikely. The chemical make up of the plants suggest they will further contaminate the atmosphere, especially if they spread.'

'But it is possible.'

'We don't know at this time, but we think it unlikely.'

'Why do you think this is the only Complex affected?'

'There is no reason we know of. You must understand, we have never encountered a new species of plant such as this one before. We are working as fast as we can to answer all the questions their appearance has raised.'

The man sat down, and another stood up and asked how many plants had been reported.

'So far seventy five have been reported, and we

have taken samples from each one,' she replied.

The presiding Officer stood up before anyone else could ask a question, told us the briefing was over, and that we were free to go. Almost immediately the sound of people talking filled the room.

'We should go,' I said to Calista, as I stood up.

She looked at me and smiled. 'I don't believe them,' she said.

'Why?'

'You said yourself that the toxin levels outside have been falling. It just seems too convenient that the plants threaten that.'

'I don't know what you mean.'

'Well, we've never been told what the safe toxin levels are, but as soon as the levels start dropping, the Officers find a reason to suggest they will rise again.'

'But if these plants are giving out toxic substances, all they can do is try and kill them.'

'Is it? What if they can't kill them? We may never be able to leave. We only have their word that they are toxic. For all we know they are cleaning up the atmosphere, or maybe the atmosphere is already clean, and nature is recovering by itself.'

'I don't know. Maybe.' I paused and thought for a moment. 'I don't see how we can find out.'

'Neither do I.'

'Let's go back to the lounge and find out what the others think.'

Bertrum and Sally had already left as we made our

way out of the room and up the stairs to the Community level and the lounge. By the time we arrived, there was a crowd of people, all talking animatedly about what we'd been told. Some, amongst the two groups that had yet to have their briefings, were listening intently to what was being said.

We found Bertrum and Sally talking to Karl and Monica. They too were discussing the plants. Karl and Monica had been in the first briefing, and had had a chance to talk about the plants with some of the other people. Karl told us that a few people were questioning the truth of what we'd been told about the plants. There was a strong feeling that we weren't being told everything. He said one person, who had studied botany in his spare time, was convinced that the plants could only grow if the atmosphere was safe for us. There was also talk of electing a group who would request more detailed information from the Officers, and report back to the rest of us. Specifically, people wanted to know more details about what the Officers considered to be safe toxin levels outside, how they thought the plants got there, and why they thought the plants posed a threat. Most people were aware the toxin levels had been falling for a long time and, like Calista, thought it too much of a coincidence that the plants had now appeared and would raise the levels again.

'Which people?' Calista asked.

'There's a group over there,' Karl said, nodding towards the far end of the room.

'I'm going to see what they have to say,' she

replied, looking at me.

'I don't think we should get involved,' I said.

'Why?'

'We don't know what the Officers might do if we cause any trouble.'

'What can they do? We are only asking for more information. It's hardly a mutiny,' Calista replied, indignantly.

'Isn't it? We've never questioned what they've told us before. Why should we now?'

'Why shouldn't we? I'm going to find out what they are saying. Are you coming?'

I looked at the others, shook my head, and said. 'Alright, I'll go with you, but just to listen. I don't think we should get involved.'

We made our way towards the group of people talking in the corner of the room. There were about forty of them. One man was addressing the crowd, while the others listened. He was talking loudly enough for us to hear what he was saying, despite us being at the back of the group. I recognised him as being one of the senior educators. He suggested, if we were interested in putting questions to the Officers, that we should hold a meeting that afternoon in one of the lecture rooms, and that we should elect a group of representatives to speak on our behalf. We could then formulate our questions and they would put them to the Officers. Most of the group agreed with his suggestions, and that he would request the use of one of the lecture rooms for later that day. As the group broke up, Calista said she wanted to go to the meeting.

'I told you, I don't want to get involved,' I said, my voice rising.

'I'm going whether you do or not,' she said.

We were walking back towards the others when we heard a shout from behind us. Four security men wearing green airspec suits had arrived, and were asking the man who had spoken to accompany them. He was resisting them, shouting that he wanted to know where they were taking him, and why. I could hear them tell him he was required in one of the Officer's consulting rooms. Most of the group had moved away from them. After a few minutes he calmed down and agreed to be taken away. There were mutterings from the rest of the group, but no one interfered as he slowly headed towards the stairs, with the security men surrounding him.

I looked at Calista, and said. 'I told you this could cause trouble.'

She looked at me, and silently continued walking back to the others.

'Karl,' Calista said, as we rejoined them, 'you've studied history. What do you know about The Collapse?'

'Probably about as much as you do. Why?'

'Tell me anyway.'

'Alright. In the mid 21st century three events conspired together to cause it. Firstly, scientists thought they had perfected ways of creating artificial life in the form of bacteria. The new bacteria were used for all sorts of things, such as attacking the immune systems of insects considered to be pests. In 2049 there was a massive oil leak in the Russian area of the Arctic Ocean, where oil had been discovered in 2032 after the ice cap had retreated due to the effects of global warming. Bacteria had been developed which were used to clean up the spill, by breaking up the oil into its constituent chemicals, so that they could be absorbed naturally in the oceans. Unfortunately, within two years a problem had arisen. The bacteria had mutated and life in the oceans wasn't regenerating. For example, fish became sterile, and plant life was dying. The oceans became toxic soups within ten years. The scientists attempted to reverse the process without success.

The second problem arose from the effect of attempting to kill off the insect pests. In some cases they also mutated, and when they fed on plant life they infected those plants. In less than fifteen years plants were dying from infections. Again, the scientists attempted to reverse the process, but it was too late. As a result, carbon dioxide levels in the atmosphere started to increase to levels the planet couldn't manage.

The third problem was the animal life. Domesticated animals bred for food were being given genetically modified food. Their yields started dropping dramatically, creating food shortages. But, the alarming problem arose in wildlife. The herbivores were being contaminated from the infected plant life. They were being eaten by the carnivores, which in turn became infected. By 2067 almost half of the wildlife had disappeared, and the plant life was reduced to eighty five percent of the levels needed to sustain the planets production of oxygen. People were eating genetically modified food as well, to supplement the reducing levels of natural food.

It was at that time that a secret group was formed, by the wealthier countries, called The Survivors Consortium. By then the scientists estimated that the planet couldn't sustain human life for more than another fifteen to twenty years. A plan was drawn up to build the Complexes, and to populate them with young healthy people who would be isolated from the outside world, in an attempt to maintain a human population. Us. The Complexes were built in isolated areas where it was considered safer. It was all done in immense secrecy. The general population was told the Complexes were to be used as an experiment for long distance space travel, and possible colonies on other planets. By 2082 they were commissioned, as billions of people around the world died from diseases contracted from infected food and, more horribly, from the increasing imbalance of carbon dioxide and other chemicals in the atmosphere, making it increasingly un-breathable. That's about all I know.'

'So the planet's ecosystems collapsed.'

'Yes. That's why it was called The Collapse. That was nearly sixty years ago.'

'What about the rain?'

'I forgot about that. Rain came from clouds which were mainly formed by evaporation from the oceans. As the water became more contaminated, so did the rainfall, and the land became even more toxic. But, as the oceans became, well thicker for want of a better word, less evaporation took place, fewer clouds were formed, and consequently less rain fell. As you know, we never see clouds in the sky now.'

'I always thought that was because of where we are. You know, a desert.'

'That's partly true, but by the time The Collapse had taken place, there was almost no non-toxic rainfall, leading to a shortage of fresh water. Initially they tried using ice from the polar caps for fresh water, but that was never going to be sustainable, and the cost was very high.'

'So The Collapse was caused by man made bacteria.'

'Basically, yes. But, from the end of the 20th century, scientists were warning their governments about global warming. Some governments took notice, but many still thought the rise in carbon dioxide levels was a normal cycle in the planet's climate. By the early part of the 21st century efforts were being made to reduce carbon dioxide emissions into the atmosphere. Most electricity was being produced by burning oil, gas and coal. As the old power stations were being decommissioned, they were being replaced by nuclear power and sustainable natural power, such as wind. However, the natural power sources were very inefficient and couldn't supply enough power for our needs. Oil was still used in some parts of the world, but it was increasingly only needed for the production of chemicals used in manufacturing. Don't forget, plastic was made from oil, so we still needed it. Most of the oil was produced in politically unstable places. When The Middle East war started in 2029 the supply of oil was cut off, and the price went up ten fold. That's when we started exploring the Arctic Ocean. Oil was found, but it was very difficult to extract. The Russian oil field was one of the more difficult ones.'

'So it was the Middle East war that started The Collapse.'

'In a way, yes. But we'd already done a massive amount of damage to the planet before then.'

'Such as?'

'Waste. At the time most plastics and man made chemicals didn't biodegrade. Attempts had been made to make them more environmentally friendly, but without any real success. The plastics had been disposed of in landfills, which were becoming ever more problematic as chemicals were used in an attempt to break them down into their constituent chemicals. The chemicals used were contaminating the planet even more. The scientists didn't fully understand how natural degradation took place, and were making things worse.'

'What caused the Middle East war?' I asked.

'There had been religious tension in the region for more than a hundred years. The Arab nations resented the Jewish people being given Palestine, which they had renamed Israel, as their homeland after the Second World War, and had tried to claim the land back for themselves on many occasions. Israel had an uneasy truce with some

Arab countries, such as Egypt, but others were very aggressive towards them. Mind you, the Israelis didn't help their cause by refusing to give the Palestinians living in Israel, their basic human rights. They effectively tried to starve them out. The old United Nations had a dilemma. Israel had been created by a United Nations Charter, and was therefore backed by them, but the international community also disliked the Israeli stance towards the Palestinians. By 2026 Iran had perfected nuclear weapons. International efforts had failed to stop them. With the building of nuclear power stations throughout the world, it was almost impossible to stop them getting nuclear material. Once they had that, it was a relatively small step to produce the enriched nuclear material needed to make weapons. In March 2029 Iran used a nuclear weapon on Israel. Israel retaliated using it's own nuclear weapons on four neighbouring countries as well as Iran. It was carnage. Israel used six, and Iran used two. The Israelis had unofficially acquired them about fifty years before. By unofficially I mean, it was thought they had them, but they had never admitted it. The threat was enough to stop its neighbours attacking, but as soon as Iran acquired them as well, the balance of power changed. The war only lasted three days, but it effectively put the Arab oilfields out of commission. The nuclear fallout didn't clear for nearly thirty years. It affected millions of square kilometres and killed millions of people in the region.'

'So it was a chain of events going back to soon after the Second World War that led to The Collapse,' I said.

'Yes, it was.'

'And here we are, nearly two hundred years later, living underground,' Sally said.

'Talking of which, do you think there will be a meeting this afternoon?' Calista asked.

'I doubt it,' I said, glancing back to where the crowd were still talking among themselves. 'We'll have to wait and see if anyone else tries to get permission to use a lecture room.'

'We could try.'

'No. Let someone else do it...'

I spent two hours during the afternoon in the fitness centre, before joining Calista in the library. She was downloading history books onto her personal workbook. She wanted to know more about the history of The Collapse and the events leading up to it. The history we were taught as children only gave us a brief outline of what had happened, and Karl's history lesson had wetted her appetite to know more.

We returned to our Multiplex at seven o'clock in the evening. There never was a meeting, and we never again saw the man who had been taken away...

Trevor William Poate

Chapter 3

Jeopardy

*I*t was nine weeks since our approval to parent. Our choices had been approved, the egg had been fertilised, and it was time for Calista to be impregnated. We were both excited. We had been to three maternity training sessions during our Community Days, and knew what to expect, but Calista was still nervous. There was a twenty percent chance of failure, despite the attention to detail and the drugs she had been taking, and would continue to take for the first week.

We'd been up since six o'clock, taking our final observation readings, prior to going to the Centre. A relief couple who would conduct Calista's classes, and manage my computer equipment, would occupy our Multiplex while we were away. They were drawn from a pool of people whose impregnation had failed, or hadn't been approved for parenting, usually for physical reasons. They would arrive after we had left, and leave before we returned the next week. We wouldn't meet them.

'Do you have everything?' I asked, as I finished my breakfast. Calista wasn't allowed any food until after the impregnation.

'Yes, I think so. Do you have the list?'

I passed her the list detailing what we would need for our week at the Centre. It was the first time either of us had spent a week away from our Multiplex since we had coupled. The list wasn't very long. It consisted mainly of toiletry items and our personal workbooks. Clean clothing would be provided for us when we arrived..

Our food would be sent to the Maternity Centre. My diet hadn't changed, but Calista's had been adjusted to improve her chances of successfully accepting the impregnation. She looked down the list.

'Yes, I've got everything.'

'Good. I'll clear up the breakfast dishes and we can go to meet the shuttle.'

'I wonder if Karl and Monica will be there this week?' she said.

'I don't know.'

Since the announcement nine weeks previously, a lot of people had been put into quarantine. Karl and Monica were two of them. The week after the announcement there had been a lot of questions asked at the briefings. The Officer's answers hadn't satisfied a small group who insisted on us being given more information about the plants. Most of them had been quarantined. Calista had wanted to ask questions as well, but I persuaded her not to get involved, for the sake of our parenting. She wasn't happy, but had agreed.

A few people had seen clouds. The problem with clouds was they were transitory. They changed shape and moved. The Officers denied their existence, which angered some people. Those people were also quarantined. We hadn't seen any clouds, and the plant outside our Multiplex had disappeared the day after we had reported it, two days after the announcement.

There was concern about the number of people being quarantined. Previously it had been a rare occurrence, but during the past nine weeks, at least ten couples had been taken away on our Community Day. There must have been others on other days.

I finished putting the dishes into the cleaner. 'We should go,' I said, giving her a hug. 'Don't worry. Everything will be alright.'

'I know, but I can't help wondering what happens to the people who are quarantined.'

'Hopefully we'll never know,' I said.

'Why do you think they never come back?'

'Perhaps they get allocated to another group of Multiplexes, and have a different Community Day.'

'Do you think so?'

'They must be somewhere. They can't just disappear.'

'Can't they?'

By this time we had arrived at the Transport room. I opened the air lock door leading to the platform and followed her through, closing it behind me. The warning light was red…

We had been told to go straight to the Maternity

Centre. Our blood checks would be done there, instead of the Medical Centre. The paediatric doctor was waiting for us as we entered the consulting room.

'Hello Calista; Callum. How are you feeling?' he said, with a smile, as we sat down.

'A little nervous,' Calista said, glancing at me.

'Don't worry. We've done these impregnations thousands of times. You'll be fine. Have you read the instructions for today?'

'Yes, we have,' I said.

'Good. We'll do your blood checks now. The results will be back with me in an hour. In the meantime one of the orderlies will show you to your accommodation. Settle yourselves in, and we'll call you when we are ready, in about two hours.'

'What happens if there is something wrong with my blood?' Calista asked.

'We'll worry about that when the time comes. But, we have no reason to think there will be a problem. Come with me and we'll take the blood now.'

We stood up and followed the doctor out of the consulting room, along the corridor and into another room where a nurse was waiting for us.

'How many women are being impregnated today?' Calista asked the doctor.

'Eight, including you.'

'Are we all grade C?'

'No. There are two grade B's, two grade D's and four grade C's.'

'Where are they?'

'They are being seen in other consulting rooms. You'll meet some of them later.'

'How long does the impregnation take?'

'About an hour. Then you will need to rest until tomorrow. Callum will be with you most of the time.'

'Will you do it?'

'Yes. There'll be another doctor and two nurses with me, but I will do the actual impregnation. Now, we need to do your blood checks,' he said, nodding to the nurse.

'Alright,' I said, as I sat down next to Calista, opposite the nurse.

We had been in the accommodation for nearly two hours when the orderly came for us. We thought we were going to the doctor's consulting room, and were surprised when we were taken to level two and shown into one of the Officer's consulting rooms.

'Good morning,' the Officer said as we entered. 'Please sit down.'

I glanced at Calista. She was looking nervous, and I was feeling nervous.

'Is there a problem?' I asked.

'I hope not,' the Officer replied. 'Tell me, Calista, why have you recently been reading history books?'

She looked at me, then turned to the Officer and said. 'I'm just curious about The Collapse and the events leading up to it.'

'We understand you were discussing it with your friends, Karl and Monica. Why was that?'

'As I said, I'm just curious. Where are Karl and Monica?'

'They're fine. We're looking after them. That's why you haven't seen them recently.'

Calista looked at me, and said. 'We thought that must be what had happened.'

'So what is the problem?' I asked.

'You must be aware that a few people have been suggesting we are being less than truthful about the discovery of the plants outside the Complex. We are just making sure that you are not among those people, before we go ahead with the impregnation,' he said, looking Calista straight in the eyes.

She looked away towards me, and said. 'But I'm just doing some reading. Why should that affect us having a child?'

'It shouldn't. But, we have to be careful for the benefit of everyone here. I'm sure you understand that. We are only interested in everyone's welfare, and the security of the Complex.'

'Calista is only doing some reading. We have no interest in causing any trouble or jeopardising the Complex,' I said. 'We just want a child.'

'What specifically do you want to know about The Collapse?' he asked.

'Just the general history. We don't get to know very much when we are children, and the subject never comes up at any other time. I'm just interested in the events leading up to it, and what the chances are that we will ever be able to go outside.'

'As you know, the scientists are constantly monitoring the situation, and will advise you when it is safe to leave,' he said.

'What about the plants? Someone said they could only grow if the atmosphere was safe,' I said.

'Who said that?' There was menace in his voice.

'I don't remember. It was someone we overheard talking about them, a few weeks ago.'

'And the clouds. If people have seen clouds, why are you denying they are there?' Calista interrupted.

'We have no record of any clouds. The people who have said they have seen them are mistaken,' he said. His voice was challenging, as though he was daring us to disagree with him. 'And why do you think it's safe outside?

'We don't know. It's just what some people are saying.'

He paused for a few moments, before saying. 'I can assure you, there is no doubt in our minds that the plants are toxic, and the atmosphere outside is still dangerous.' His voice had changed, to an almost soothing level.

'So why do people keep getting quarantined?'

'Quarantined? Why do you think people are being quarantined?'

'We thought they were,' I said.

'No. You're mistaken. Some people have been reassigned to different Multiplexes and Community Days. It sometimes happens. A few people do get quarantined, but not many, and not very often. There's nothing sinister in that. It's for their own welfare.'

'I suppose so,' Calista said, glancing at me.

'Were Karl and Monica quarantined?' I asked.

'You don't need to worry about them, and it would be better for you both, not to discuss the plants with other people, or doubt what you've been told,' he said. It sounded like a threat.

'Yes, alright.' I said, wondering what would happen if we did.

'Alright. You should return to the Maternity Centre. Someone will be along to see you soon.'

'Does that mean we can go ahead with the impregnation?' I said.

'We'll let you know shortly.'

Calista and I stood up and began to leave. 'What happens to the people who get quarantined?' she said, as we reached the door.

'We look after them. Now, you should go.'

We waited in the accommodation for another hour, unsure if we would be allowed to continue with the impregnation, before an orderly came for us. He took us to the doctor's consulting room where we were told the impregnation would take place during the afternoon. We both breathed a sigh of relief.

Trevor William Poate

We were taken for the impregnation at three o'clock, and I was allowed to watch from a viewing room. The two doctors, and two nurses, worked quickly and efficiently as the procedure took place. Calista was mildly anaesthetised, but was still awake during the hour it took, and appeared comfortable throughout. Afterwards she was taken to a small recovery room to rest for the night. I was allowed to see her briefly, before going back to the accommodation to have some food in the feeding room.

The other seven 'fathers' were there, all as excited as I was. It wasn't very often I had a chance to talk at length with anyone from a different grade because our Community Days were graded, and I took the opportunity to find out as much as I could about their lives in the Complex. Surprisingly, they all wanted to talk about the plants, and what was happening outside. I remembered what the Officer had said, but thought there was no harm in the discussion. One of the grade D people, Colin, told us he had been outside to collect the plants. He explained he had to wear an isolation suit with his own oxygen pack, and that he was only allowed out for thirty minutes at a time. I asked him about the conditions outside. He couldn't tell us very much, other than the ground was made up of small granules of stone called sand, which he sank into when he walked. It sounded exactly as I expected, judging from what I'd seen from our Observation room. He told us the plants were becoming more common. They weren't very big, around a metre high, and were covered in sharp points which he had been warned to avoid touching in case his suit was compromised. He said he'd been out twenty times and collected nearly fifty samples. We asked him what happened to them, but all he knew was they were put into a sealed container and then taken to one of the science laboratories. I found it surprising that no one considered the appearance of the plants to be anything other than unusual. I didn't suggest anything else, but wondered about their lack of concern.

I spent a comfortable night in the accommodation, and was dressed and ready for breakfast by seven o'clock. The doctor had told me the previous day that I could spend time with Calista, after she had been allowed out of the recovery room and back into our accommodation. She needed to rest for another twenty-four hours, after which she would be allowed to go to the Community room. She would have tests every day to make sure the impregnation was going normally, and we would return to our Multiplex on our next Community Day, six days away.

Colin was in the feeding room when I arrived. I collected my breakfast and sat down next to him. He was curiously silent.

'We shouldn't talk about the plants anymore,' he eventually said, as I started eating.

'Why?'

'I had a visit from one of the Officers after we went back to the accommodation last night. He wanted to know why we were talking about the plants. He was quite threatening. He told me not to talk about them again.'

'But we were only chatting.'

'I know. But he suggested it wasn't too late to abort the impregnation if I didn't keep quiet.'

I didn't know what to say. I was shocked that we were being listened to, and wondered if I would be warned as well.

'How did he know what we were talking about?'

'I don't know. He didn't say, but I don't want to risk the impregnation,' he said, glancing around the room.

We were the only people there, apart from the feeding staff. I wondered if we were still being listened to, or if one of the others had told the Officers about our conversation.

'Have you seen any of the others this morning? I asked.

'No. They had already left by the time I got here.'

'Do you think one of them reported you?'

'I don't know, and I don't want to talk about it anymore.'

I continued eating in silence.

He finished his breakfast and stood up to leave. 'Be careful,' he said, quietly.

I looked at him, wondering again if we were being overheard. 'I will,' I said.

I finished my breakfast, cleared away my dishes, and went back to the accommodation. I wasn't due to see Calista for another hour. I spent the time debating with myself about whether I should tell her what had happened.

I decided I would, when I thought it was safe to do so.

I was about to leave when there was a knock on the door. An orderly was standing outside. He told me I was wanted in the recovery room straight away.

'Is everything alright?' I asked him.

'I don't know. I was just told to come and get you.'

We hurried along the corridor to Calista's room. She was sitting up in bed and had obviously been crying. There was a nurse standing alongside the bed, and a security man standing by the door.

'What's happened?' I asked, sitting on the bed and giving her a hug.

'I've lost the baby,' she cried.

I was stunned. 'How, I mean, what happened?'

'I started bleeding two hours ago, just after breakfast, and aborted it,' she said, glancing at the nurse.

'What happened?' I said to the nurse.

'There's always a chance the impregnation won't take. You were told that,' she said.

'I know, but I didn't think…'

'The doctor will be here in a minute. He'll explain everything to you,' she said, interrupting me. She didn't seem very sympathetic.

I held Calista closely until the doctor arrived, a few minutes later.

'Calista; Callum. I'm sorry about the baby. Unfortunately you won't be able to have another one,' he said, in a blunt, offhand, manner.

Trevor William Poate

'Why?' I said.

'An Officer will be along soon to explain the situation to you, and what will happen next.'

'What do you mean?' I said. Calista was crying again.

'He'll tell you. That's all I can say at the moment.'

It was clear he wasn't going to tell us any more. I just sat, holding Calista, trying to comfort her. She was by now sobbing, almost uncontrollably.

We waited nearly ten minutes before the Officer arrived; the one who had interrogated us the day before. He came in and sat on one of the chairs opposite the bed.

'I'm sorry about the pregnancy,' he said. 'We were concerned about you both after the interview yesterday morning, but decided to allow the impregnation to take place. Unfortunately, that decision was reversed because of your conversation with the other fathers yesterday evening, Callum. The decision was taken to abort the foetus this morning.'

'Why? We were only talking' I said, standing up over him, clenching my fists.

The security man came towards me, ready to intervene.

'Please calm down. Getting angry won't help. The decision wasn't taken lightly.'

'What happens now?'

'You are going to be reassigned to the Relief group, and given a new Multiplex and Community Day.'

'But we don't want to be reassigned.'

'You don't have a choice. The reassignment will take place tomorrow, when Calista is sufficiently recovered to leave here.'

'Will we be together?'

'Yes, you will.'

'What were you talking about?' Calista said to me, in a broken voice.

'We were just talking about the plants. There was nothing to it. It was just talk,' I said, sitting back down on the bed and holding her more tightly. 'We did nothing wrong.'

'We don't see it like that,' the Officer said.

'Did you force the abortion?'

'Yes. It was something we added to Calista's breakfast.'

'That's murder,' Calista screamed.

'No. It's self preservation. We cannot allow anyone to jeopardise the future of the Complex.'

'Jeopardise! How have we jeopardised the Complex?' I said.

'I can't say any more, but I suggest you forget about trying to find out any more about The Collapse, or the plants, for your own good.' His voice was threatening. 'I did warn you yesterday morning.'

'And if we don't?'

'We'll have to look after you.'

'You mean we'll be quarantined?'

'I'll leave you both now. Just remember what I've said. We are only thinking about the welfare of everyone in the Complex, including you,' he said, ignoring my question.

The security man escorted us back to the accommodation room early in the afternoon. He told us we would have to stay there for the rest of the day, and that food would be brought to us later.

I tried to comfort Calista, but she was distraught. I didn't know what to say to her. She blamed me for the abortion, and lay silently on the bed for most of the afternoon, occasionally sleeping. I was angry with myself and the Officers, and determined to find out what was really happening with the plants, the clouds, and outside. I was convinced the Officers weren't telling us the truth. I couldn't believe a harmless conversation had led to the abortion.

An orderly brought us food late in the afternoon. Neither of us was hungry, and when he returned to collect the dishes he warned us we would get into trouble if we didn't eat anything. We both ate a small amount, which seemed to satisfy him, and he took the dishes away.

The Officer arrived soon after, accompanied by a security man, and told us we would start two days retraining the next morning at nine o'clock. Someone would come and collect us after breakfast, which he strongly advised us to eat.

'What will happen to our belongings in our Multiplex?' I asked him.

'We will move them to your new Multiplex. You

will move there in three days. Your reassignment will commence two days after that. You will be given all the details tomorrow,' he said, before leaving us alone again.

We slept fitfully, Calista crying most of the night, while I lay there wondering what we should do.

We were both awake early the next morning. Calista was still upset, but sufficiently composed to talk.

'I'm sorry,' I said for the umpteenth time. 'I never dreamt this would happen.'

'I know. I probably would have done the same as you did. It was only a conversation,' she said, hugging me. 'We have to find out the truth.'

'I've been thinking that. But, how?'

'I don't know. Maybe some people on our new Community Day will know. I can't help wondering what happens to the people who are quarantined. Perhaps that is the answer.'

'What do you mean?'

'Unless the Officers murder them, they must be somewhere.'

'But they can't murder them all, surely? That's ridiculous.'

'They murdered our baby.'

We stood silently for a few moments, holding each other.

'And what happens to the parents? Why do they all die so young?' she said, breaking away, and looking in my eyes.

'I don't know, but we have to find out.'

'I don't want to be reassigned. Perhaps we can persuade them to let us go back to our old work and Multiplex.'

'We can try,' I said, thinking it unlikely.

An orderly came for us just before nine o'clock, and took us to the training room. The room was on level four and was equipped with tables and computer terminals. Colin was there, with Alicia, his partner.

'What are you doing here?' I asked. I hadn't expected to see him again.

'We lost our baby,' Alicia said. 'They murdered him. They said we were subversive because Colin was talking about the plants.' She was obviously upset.

'They murdered our baby as well,' Calista said, her voice breaking.

'We should talk,' I said.

'What about? The Officers control us,' Colin replied, angrily. 'They won't tell us anything. We are like dolls, or puppets, and they hold the strings.'

I was about to reply when an adult educator, a security man, and an Officer entered the room.

'Good morning everyone. This is Sofia. She will be instructing you over the next two days,' the Officer said, gesturing to the woman standing next to him, 'and my name is Johannes.'

'Instructing us in what?' I said.

'Instructing you in your new work,' he replied.

'I don't want to change my work. I want to go back to my old work,' Calista said, in a shrill voice.

Johannes looked at Sofia and said. 'I'm afraid that is not possible.'

'Why not? I haven't done anything wrong.'

'That's not my decision.'

'Yes it is. You're an Officer. You make all the decisions.'

'No I don't. The decision was made by other Officers. Not by me.'

'Then I want to speak with them.'

'That won't be possible.'

'In that case I want to be quarantined.'

I looked at Calista in amazement. It hadn't crossed my mind that she would say that.

'Why? Are you ill?' Johannes said.

'No. But I'm not going to co-operate anymore.'

'Calista,' I said. 'Please don't be difficult.'

'You should listen to Callum. He obviously knows what's best for you,' Sofia said to Calista.

'No I don't know what's best for her,' I said angrily. 'but I don't want her to disappear, either.'

'What do you mean, disappear?'

'That's what happens to people when they are quarantined. Isn't it?'

Colin and Alicia had remained silent throughout our arguing. 'What does happen to people when they are quarantined?' Colin said.

'We look after them,' Johannes replied.

Trevor William Poate

'What does that mean?' Alicia said.

'I can't tell you any more than that.'

'In that case I'm not going to co-operate either. If the only way to find out what happens when people are quarantined is to be quarantined, then I want to be quarantined as well. I don't want to be reassigned either.'

'Neither do I,' Colin said.

I looked at them all, surprised at what they'd said. 'And neither do I,' I said.

'You don't have any other option than reassignment,' Johannes replied, glancing at Sofia.

'But if we refuse to co-operate, what else can you do?' Calista said.

'You must co-operate. It's that simple.'

'No. It isn't.'

By this time we were standing face to face. The security man started to move towards us, anticipating trouble.

Johannes looked at Sofia, concern on his face, and said. 'Wait here. I'll be back in a while.'

Sofia smiled at him as he left the room. 'What did you do to be reassigned?' she asked me when he'd gone.

'We talked about the plants.'

'I see. What did you say?'

'We just chatted about them. There was nothing in it.'

'But you must have said something they don't like.'

'I don't know. All I know is they aborted Calista

and Alicia's babies.'

'I was studying The Collapse,' Calista said.

'They don't like people who do that.'

'Why? It's only history?'

'They just don't…'

'Then they shouldn't give us access to the history books.'

'No, they shouldn't.'

Johannes returned about half an hour later with three more security men.

'We're sending you back to your accommodation until a decision is made,' he said.

'What sort of decision?' Calista asked.

'A decision about your future. That's all I can tell you.'

'All I want is to go back to my old work and Multiplex, and be allowed to parent.'

'I'm sorry, but that is not an option.'

'Then I want to be quarantined.'

'That is not an option either. You need to go now. The security men will go with you,' he said, nodding to the four men.

We didn't struggle, or cause any trouble, as the security men led us away. There wasn't any point. We would just have to wait to hear our fate.

Food was brought to us by an orderly at lunch time. We ate in silence, wondering when we would be recalled to the training room. Apart from the security man outside the door, and the orderly bringing more food and collecting our dishes, we saw no one else that day.

It seemed to last forever...

Chapter 4

Quarantine

*J*ohannes and another Officer arrived at ten o'clock, and entered our accommodation room with the security man from outside our door. They sat down in two of the chairs alongside the table and gestured for us to do the same, while the security man stood by the door.

'Colin and Alicia have seen sense, and agreed to be reassigned,' Johannes said. 'We'd like you to do the same.'

I looked at Calista. We had spent most of the previous day talking about whether we should agree to be reassigned. We had finally agreed that if we couldn't return to our old work and Multiplex, we wouldn't agree to it, but were worried about what being quarantined meant..

'I don't believe you,' I said.

'What you believe doesn't matter. I'm telling you they have agreed to be reassigned.'

'What did you do to them?' My voice was rising in anger.

'We didn't do anything to them. We just persuaded them they would be better agreeing to the reassignment,' he said, calmly.

'How?'

'By speaking with them the same as we are with you.'

'We want to go back to our old work and Multiplex,' Calista said, in an emotional voice, 'and be allowed to parent.'

'That is not an option.'

'Then we want to be quarantined,' I said, trying to keep my voice calm.

Johannes looked at the other Officer, nodded, and said. 'We had hoped you would see sense as well. You don't understand what being quarantined means, and I can't tell you. But, if you insist we will arrange it, although you may regret it. We prefer people to be reassigned.' It sounded like a threat.

'Tell us what it means,' I said.

'I can't do that. Once you have been quarantined you can't go back. You will not return to your old work, or Multiplex.'

'But we can't go back anyway,' Calista said.

'No, you can't. But you can be reassigned.'

Calista looked at me and said. 'No, we want to go back, or be quarantined.'

Johannes and the other Officer, who hadn't said anything, stood up and made their way to the door. 'Alright,' Johannes said, 'we'll come back later. Be ready to leave.'

The security man also left the room. We were

alone again.

'Do you think quarantine means death?' Calista said. She was shaking.

'I don't know what it means,' I replied, quietly. 'We'll find out soon...'

We packed our belongings in the small black plastic cases we had brought from our Multiplex. Johannes returned about two hours later.

'Are you ready?' he asked as he entered the room.

I looked at Calista, and said. 'Yes, we are.'

'You can still change your mind,' he said.

'No. We don't want to.'

'Alright. Follow me.'

We left the room and followed him, with the security man, to level one. We'd never been there before, and were surprised to find it had windows similar to our Observation room, and we could see outside.

'Where are we going?' I asked.

'Just follow me. You'll find out soon enough.'

We walked for about ten minutes before stopping at an air lock. Johannes pressed a button and the door opened. We entered, and he closed the door behind us before pressing another button, which opened a door to reveal a shuttle waiting for us.

'I'll leave you here,' he said. 'When the shuttle stops, someone will meet you and escort you to the Quarantine Centre, where you will be looked after.'

I looked at Calista. She was shaking again.

Trevor William Poate

'What do you mean, 'looked after'?' I said.

'You'll find out when you get there.'

'Why can't you tell us now?'

'For security reasons.'

'Whose security?'

'The security of the Complex. That's all I can tell you. Now, get in the shuttle. It's ready to leave.'

He obviously wasn't going to tell us anything, so I took Calista's hand and we went inside. The door closed behind us as we sat down, and it started to move. Both of us were shaking, with fear and trepidation.

It was a long journey, lasting nearly two hours. When the shuttle stopped and the door opened, we were met by a security man who told us to follow him.

'Where are we?' I asked him.

'This is the Quarantine Centre,' he said.

'Yes, but where are we?'

'You'll find out soon,' he replied.

We walked for a few minutes along a windowless corridor, carrying our bags, before the security man stopped at a door, pressed a button and waited until the green light alongside lit up. The door opened and he gestured for us to enter.

We went inside where there were two women and two men sitting behind a long table. There were two chairs in front, which they pointed to, suggesting we should sit down. We went over, and sat down. Unusually they were all wearing white airspec suits.

'Callum; Calista. Welcome to the Quarantine Centre,' one of the women said.

'Where are we?' I asked.

'This is a remote part of the Complex, a long way from the Centre and the Multiplexes,' the woman replied.

'Are you Officers?'

'Not exactly. Our position is better described as Facilitators. Consider this as somewhere you are out of harm's way.'

'What happens here?'

'You'll be told all you need to know in due course. In the meantime, we want to know what you know about The Collapse.'

I looked at Calista. 'Not very much really,' I said.

'I've been doing some reading, but I don't know a great deal either,' Calista said.

'We'd like you to tell us what you do know. Take your time.'

We spent the next two hours telling them what we knew. They occasionally asked questions, but listened silently most of the time, and took notes on their workbooks. When we finished they thanked us for our honesty, and told us we would be taken to an accommodation area for the rest of the day, and food would be brought to us. The woman, who seemed to be in charge, told us we would be collected the following morning, and told about the Quarantine Centre. They didn't invite questions, and we were too nervous and confused to ask any. Just as we left she told us not to worry, and that nothing bad was going to happen to us.

The accommodation was very different from our Multiplex. We had a living area; a bedroom, a bathroom, and a room with equipment we didn't recognise. The furniture was similar to that we had in our Multiplex, but there was more of it.

We were surprised to find our personal belongings had been moved from our Multiplex. We clearly weren't returning there. The biggest surprise was the windows.

'This is very strange,' I said to Calista.

'Yes, but those people, the Facilitators, seemed friendly,' she replied, gazing out of one of the windows into the distance.

I went over to where she was standing and looked out of the window. All I could see was the shuttle tube, above ground, snaking away into the distance over the yellowish brown earth. The accommodation was three levels up, and gave us views further than we had ever seen before.

'Judging by the time it took to get here, we must be about sixty or seventy kilometres from the Centre,' I said.

'I wonder why we are so far away.'

'I don't know. I suppose we'll find out tomorrow.'

We both turned away and went to sit on the soft armchairs in the living area. It was strange sitting in a room lit by natural light. Our Multiplex had been lit artificially. The only time we'd seen sunlight was during the time we'd spent in our Observation room.

Trevor William Poate

71

'Did you notice the colour of their skins? They were light brown,' Calista said.

'Yes. I did,' I replied, looking at her white hands and face. 'We'd better unpack.'

An orderly brought us food later in the day, and returned for the dishes an hour later. He also brought us a supply of white airspec suits and told us we would be using them instead of our blue ones from now on. We saw no one else until the following morning.

The sunlight streaming through the windows woke us early the next morning. It was strange being woken by natural light. In the Multiplex we relied on the alarm at six o'clock every morning, indicating it was time to get up. Here, the sunlight woke us at six o'clock. I'd stayed up late the previous evening, gazing out at the stars twinkling in the clear, black, night sky. Even more amazing was the moon. It wasn't completely round and was much brighter than I expected. It must have been only part of the way through it's monthly cycle, but it held my attention anyway. I'd never seen the moon or stars before, neither had Calista. There was a lot we hadn't seen.

The orderly brought us breakfast and told us we had an hour before being collected for our first briefing. I asked him what the briefing was about, but he said he couldn't tell me. I wondered if he couldn't, or wouldn't, but it didn't matter. We'd soon find out.

At exactly eight o'clock we were taken down one floor to a small room where there were ten or eleven tables with computers. The sign on the door said 'Training Room 7'. There were four other people already there, and two more joined us soon after. One of the women who had interviewed us the previous day was standing at the front, behind a table, looking at her workbook She had short black hair, wore a white airspec suit the same as ours, and was probably in her mid thirties. We sat down behind one of the tables and silently waited for her to speak.

'Good morning everyone,' she said, once we'd settled. 'Before we start I'll introduce you to each other. You'll be spending a lot of time together. Firstly, my name is Patricia, I am in charge of your retraining.'

'Retraining for what?' a man sitting in front of me asked.

'Please let me finish,' she said. She introduced us to each other, and asked each of us to tell the others what our work had been in the Complex. We spoke in turn. There were four teachers: Kevin, Liam, Tina and Calista, three technicians: Fabio, Abigail and me, and a nurse, Julia. We were all of a similar age, and none of us had children.

'People are brought here because they have questioned the honesty, and authority, of the Officers in the Complex, become ill, reached retirement age, or perhaps simply become problematical. Your days in the Complex are numbered. During the course of the next month you will be trained in self sufficiency, in preparation for leaving here. You will then spend a month in a Rehabilitation Centre, where you will be taught how to live outside. You will also be taught the purpose of the Complex, it's history, and what is happening outside.'

There were murmurs among us.

'How can we leave the Complex? It's toxic outside,' Julia, the nurse, said.

'I'll explain that to you this morning.'

'Why is this called the Quarantine Centre?' I asked.

'Please. No more questions at the moment, there'll be plenty of time for them, later.'

We fell silent for a few moments, as she tapped at the screen of her workbook and put a picture on the large screen on the wall behind her.

'This Complex, and the other nine around the world, was first occupied in 2082. They were built by 'The Survivors Consortium' in an attempt to ensure the survival of the human race. At the time, scientists believed the planet's ecosystems were collapsing, hence 'The Collapse'. However, that wasn't the case. On the contrary, the planet was recovering naturally, and within five years of the Complexes opening it was realised they were unnecessary. The Consortium's investment in the Complexes was enormous. They decided, that instead of wasting their investment, they would use the Complexes as an experiment in eugenics. For those of you unsure what that means, it is essentially selective breeding in humans.'

She paused for a few moments while what she had said sank in with us.

'What do you mean by 'experiment'?' Calista said, her voice rising.

'Please be calm Calista,' she said.

'Calm? How can I be calm when you've just told me I'm a manufactured freak?'

'I didn't say that. You are a normal human being. The only difference is that your parentage was determined by scientists, and that minor changes were made to decide some of your genetic characteristics. Nothing was done that couldn't happen naturally.'

'Naturally? How can choosing someone's interests, or, or eye colour, before they are even conceived, be called natural?'

'Please, calm down and listen to me. Nothing has been done to harm anyone. You are all perfectly normal. Let me explain. The experiment was designed in such a way as to simulate possible colonising of the moon, or even other planets. It was determined that for it to work it must be shrouded in secrecy, especially from the people living in the Complexes. It was, and is, important that everyone here believes that the outside is toxic, incapable of supporting human life.'

There were more murmurs around the room. She raised her hand to quieten us, and continued.

'In order to maintain a static population, and breed new generations, people attaining approximately forty five years of age are brought here, retrained in the skills they need to live outside, and released. That is why there are almost no elderly people in the Complex, apart from some

Officers. People who become ill, or in some other way become a threat to the Complex, are brought here and retrained in the same way as you will be. We almost never bring individuals, only couples. That is why you are all here.'

'What happens to single people?' Abigail asked.

'They are encouraged to couple, and conform. So far they nearly all have,' Patricia replied.

By this time, my head was spinning with questions, and Calista was staring into space, dumbfounded. The consequences of what we had been told were enormous. We were artificial, just an experiment to amuse The Consortium, or so it seemed to me.

'Your retraining will equip you to live among the general population. The training will cover all aspects of your new life outside. You will also be given somewhere to live, and work to do. Crucially, to some of you, your sterilisation will be reversed, allowing you to have children naturally.'

Calista looked at me and smiled.

'You should be aware of the importance of the work done in the Complexes. You, and all the other people, have helped scientists understand the effects of genetic engineering, and to improve the quality and length of life of the people living outside. We also do a lot of work on plants and animals, but you'll find out about that later on. Many of the mistakes made by scientists, at the end of the last century, have been reversed. Disease and famine have almost been eradicated and the planet's ecosystems have been stabilised. Finally, you must understand that when you leave here, you must not talk about the Complexes to anyone. You will be monitored, your behaviour watched, and any indiscretions dealt with. This is a once only chance for each of you.'

She looked at each of us in turn, attempting to gauge our response to what she had told us.

'There is one other thing you should know. Each of you has an identical twin. Part of the experiment requires each mother to give birth to two children at a time. You have been kept here, in the Complex, and your twin, sent outside. This has been done so that we can compare the development, both physically and mentally, of each of you.'

She stopped speaking, sensing the tension in the room.

I noticed Julia give Kevin a strange look, a look suggesting they already knew about the twins.

'Will I meet my twin?' Abigail asked.

'No, you won't. None of you will.'

She paused and looked at each of us in turn.

'I'm going to leave you for a while. You can discuss amongst yourselves what I've told you and, after lunch, I will answer your questions. Your retraining will start tomorrow.'

She left the room before any of us could speak. Almost immediately, after she had gone, everyone started talking at once. After a few minutes, I stood up, walked to the front of the room, and said. 'Listen everyone. I think it would be best if we worked together, list out our questions, and after lunch put them to her. If we do that, we'll waste less time talking across each other, and find out more. Does everyone agree?'

Fabio stood up and said. 'Alright, who wants to take down the questions?'

'I will, if you like,' I said. Everyone in the room nodded agreement. 'We'd better start then. I suggest each of you tell us what you want to know, individually, and I'll compile the questions...'

By lunchtime, two hours later, I had nearly fifty questions we wanted to ask. I'd grouped them into five categories. I guessed some of them would be covered by the answers given to others, so didn't expect to have to ask them all.

An orderly took us to a feeding room for our lunch. The food was the same reconstituted paste we ate in our Multiplexes, and I wondered if we would eventually eat real, natural, food. I added the question to my list.

'I told you the Officers weren't telling us the truth,' Calista said, as we started eating. 'We're nothing but...but, synthetic.'

'I know, and you were right,' I replied, taking her hand and squeezing it. 'But, we'll be alright together. I promise.'

Patricia came for us soon after we'd finished eating. She was accompanied by one of the men who had interviewed Calista and me the previous day. We followed them back to the training room where she asked us if we were ready.

I stood up and said we had a long list of questions, which I would ask on behalf of everyone. She nodded her agreement before introducing the man. She told us his name was Ronaldo, that he would assist her in our retraining over the next month, and would help her answer our questions. He was about the same age as Patricia, tall with black curly hair, and swarthy skin much darker than hers, but not black.

I explained I had put the questions into five categories, told her what they were, and asked her if she had a preference to the order I asked them.

'No. Any order you like,' she said.

I took a deep breath and asked the first question…

After four hours of heated discussion, we had finished. I asked the others if they had any more questions they wanted to ask, but none were forthcoming. Everyone seemed both numb, and elated, at the thought of our future freedom.

Patricia told us we would have plenty of opportunities to ask further questions, as they arose, over the following two months. Finally she gave each of us a new workbook.

'Everything you need to know during your retraining is on these workbooks. As we proceed through the retraining, we will tell you which pages to read, and their access codes. You cannot access anything without the appropriate code, so don't bother trying.'

Before she left she told us we would eat dinner in the same place we'd eaten lunch, and that there was a recreation room available to us next door to it. There was also a fitness room further along the corridor. Finally, she told us we would start our retraining the following morning at eight o'clock, and gave us the page number and access code on our workbooks for the following week's schedule.

'I wonder where our twins are, and what they are doing,' Calista said, as we prepared for bed.

'I don't know. I don't suppose we ever will know,' I replied.

'You're probably right. But I'd still like to know.'

'Yes. So would I. I'd also like to know where our parents are.'

I spent a long time gazing at the stars and the moon that night, as they moved slowly across the sky, wondering what the outside world was like, while Calista slept restlessly in my arms.

Chapter 5

Retraining

*R*onaldo and Patricia shared the first week's training between them. We were taught the history of the world since the Complexes had been opened, history denied to anyone living in them for nearly sixty years. The documented history we knew had stopped at 2082, but so much had happened since, we were amazed.

The scare of human extinction after the expected Collapse, had unified governments around the world. There was still some dissent, but essentially agreements had been reached. The world was now grouped into eight Regional Federations, loosely based on continental geography, with a central government based in India. Patricia put a map of the regions on the screen behind her. Only Asia was split into more than one Federation. The Far East: Central Asia, and The Middle East. Africa: North America, South and Central America, Australasia and Europe, were the others.

What had once been countries were now states with representatives appointed to the eight Regional Governments. People lived anywhere they wanted within their region, removing border conflicts and potential fighting, although there were still a few religious disputes, mainly over religious sites. The world's population had stabilised at just over ten billion people, the most the planet could sustain, even with genetically modified food.

There was an international military. Weapons of mass destruction had been eradicated after the accidental detonation of a nuclear weapon in China in 2098 which killed thirteen million people. Everyone had at last seen sense. The military were used simply to police the few people living outside of one of the Federations and the occasional, mostly religious, disputes. The people living outside were known as Renegades, and were largely left alone.

Nuclear power was still the main source of electricity, but new natural methods had been developed, using the thermal energy of the planet, and energy from the sun collected, as we had done, by photoelectric cells, though much more efficiently than the old ones used in the Complexes.

The scientists had stabilised the world's ecosystems, and global warming had been reversed, as carbon dioxide and methane levels in the atmosphere were reduced.

The world's economy was also centralised in India. There was no money. Everyone earned credits according to their grade, which was a similar grading system to the one used in the Complex. We had never earned credits, and the concept of paying for things was hard to grasp. Everything we needed in the Complex had been provided. People had registration cards which held their credits and bio data, but were not micro chipped like us. They used the credits to purchase goods, such as clothing and food. Services, such as electricity, water, hospitals, schooling, and accommodation were provided free of charge, according to each person's grade. The credits given to people within each grade were almost the same throughout the world. Ronaldo told us this helped reduce the temptation to move from one area to another for credit benefits. If people did want to move they needed to find someone to exchange with. The Regional Governments provided exchange databases to facilitate the moves. People were not encouraged to move outside of their own region, but could visit other regions during an annual vacation period. We didn't know what a vacation was, and when he explained, it didn't make sense why people would want to spend time doing nothing!

The Survivors Consortium still existed, and was still secret. They were concerned about people fearing it would be used to create a 'Super Race'. I didn't feel very super, neither did Calista. Ronaldo and Patricia spent a lot of time explaining the importance of the work being done by The Consortium, and the importance of maintaining it's secrecy. The experiment still bothered me, especially the secrecy, and nearly thirty thousand people living a lie.

And there were plants, animals and clouds, but not where our Complex was.

By the end of the first week we had been given so much information, our heads ached. We were given a day off to rest before starting to learn about our new lifestyles.

'I've been thinking,' Calista said, on the morning of our rest day. 'Everything seems so controlled. I know we are used to that, but I thought that when we were allowed out, we would have our freedom. I rather like the idea of becoming a Renegade.'

'I'm not so sure. I rather like the idea of the security we are being given. Not having to concern ourselves about where to live and work, or our food.'

'But it seems to me that almost the only difference between the outside and the Complex is; being outside.'

'And breathing fresh air, and eating real food, and…and having our own family.'

She went quiet for a while.

'When do you think our sterilisation will be reversed?' she eventually said.

'Before we leave here, I suppose.'

'And real food. When do you think we will be able to try that?'

'I don't know. Soon I expect. Our bodies will need to adapt to the food and we'll need to learn how to prepare it.'

'I wonder what it tastes like.'

'I wonder what it tastes and feels like. I know we've seen pictures, but they don't really tell us very much, other than that it comes in lots of different shapes, colours, and sizes.'

'I want to see animals.'

'Do you think it's right to eat animals?'

Trevor William Poate

'I don't know. I can't imagine what they taste like.'

Calista walked over towards one of the windows, gazed out, and said. 'There's so much to find out.'

I joined her, put my arms around her waist, and said. 'I know, but we'll manage. You'll see.'

We spent a couple of hours in the fitness room in the afternoon, before joining the rest of the group for our evening meal. We had become friendly with all of them during our first week, and had some interesting conversations about what we'd learned. It had been useful talking with them during the evenings. There had been so much information that none of us had taken it all in the first time we heard it. Our discussions helped by reminding each other what we'd been told, and listening to different interpretations of some of the information. Fabio and Tina seemed to remember more than the rest of us. They seemed to have photographic memories!

During our meal, Ronaldo joined us and told us the workbook page number and access code for our itinerary for the following two weeks. He also told us he was showing a holographic in the cinema room that evening, a holographic he thought we should watch, although we didn't have to. We were intrigued, so we all decided to attend the viewing.

Our itinerary for the two weeks was loosely entitled 'Life Support'. He explained it consisted of learning about the different types of food we would have available to us outside, and how we could prepare it. At the end of the training we would be expected to prepare food for ourselves, and occasionally for the group, until we finished our month in the Quarantine Centre. We would also be taught about the nutritional value of the food, and the importance of maintaining a balanced diet.

The holographic turned out to be fascinating. None of us had given any thought to community living. We were so used to living in our Multiplexes during the week and only meeting people on our Community Days, that the concept of seeing people at work, and in our spare time, was alien. The previous week was the first time we'd spent more than one day at a time with a group of people. The holographic described the responsibilities of community living, and used interviews with people, from example communities, to explain what we should expect. The apparent lack of privacy was disconcerting. The holographic showed us the type of accommodation we could expect to live in, and shops. We knew about shops, but the idea of being able to choose what we ate, our clothing, and so many other things, in a crowd of people doing the same thing, was almost frightening.

It only lasted two hours, but gave us an amazing insight into what we should expect when we left the Complex. We talked about it as a group for nearly an hour, before Ronaldo told us we should return to our accommodations, because we would need to be up early for the next day's training. We were meeting at seven o'clock, he said, with breakfast at six, because we had a trip to make.

    'Where are we going?' Abigail asked.

    'You'll find out in the morning,' he replied.

    The stars were twinkling again that night, and the pale yellow moon was nearly a full circle, eerily lighting up the orange landscape outside.

Chapter 6

Sustenance

*P*atricia joined us for our early breakfast and, when we had finished eating, told us to meet at the shuttle entrance just before seven o'clock.

'Don't be late,' she said. 'The shuttle is booked for us, and we can't miss it.'

Ronaldo was waiting with her when we arrived. We were the first, and asked where we were going.

'We'll tell you during the journey,' Ronaldo said, glancing at Patricia, mysteriously.

The shuttle warning light was still red when the last of the group arrived. We waited in anticipation, wondering where we were going, and why. It turned yellow, and then green as the door opened.

The shuttle compartment was empty as we entered and sat down. The air lock door closed, then the shuttle door, and we felt it move off.

'Open page F151a on your workbooks. That will explain where we are going, and why,' she said. 'The access code is P72D/1.'

'How long is the journey?' Julia asked.

'About an hour,' Patricia replied.

We opened our workbooks and accessed the page.

We were going to the Flora Centre, it told us, where we would learn about plants.

We were talking amongst ourselves when the shuttle came to a stop. We had tried to ask Ronaldo and Patricia some questions, but they both declined to answer, saying we would find out all we needed to know during the visit, and over the following two weeks.

The shuttle door opened, and a middle-aged woman met us. She briefly spoke with Patricia, before telling us to follow her. She took us to a training room equipped with computers, tables and a large display screen hanging on a wall, similar to the training room in the Quarantine Centre.

'Good morning,' she said, after we had sat down. 'My name is Rose and I manage The Flora Centre. Before I show you around I want to explain what we do here, and the basics of how it works.

You have been told about the eugenics part of The Experiment. The Flora Centre is the part dealing with genetically modified plants. There are three main studies. The first deals with improving the ability of plants to convert carbon dioxide into oxygen, the second deals with improving yields of plants used for food, and the third deals with naturally produced chemicals used in medicines.'

She paused for a few moments, glancing at each of us in turn, before continuing.

'It became obvious to scientists in the late 21st

century that for the planet to sustain life, the plants, mainly trees, would need to become more efficient at producing oxygen and reducing carbon dioxide in the atmosphere, particularly as the human population grew at the expense of vegetation. During the past fifty years the experiments conducted here have improved their efficiency by nearly fifteen percent.

In 2105, when the Federations were established, each region was tasked with allocating areas to be used for reafforestation, and for wild animals. The scientists working for the Central Government had determined that at least forty percent of the planet's cultivated land needed to be allowed to grow wild. Much of the allocated land has since been managed and planted with modified vegetation first grown here. The results have been dramatic. Global warming, as a result of excess carbon dioxide and methane in the atmosphere, has been reversed and the ice caps over the north and south poles are beginning to return to the levels they were in the mid 21st century.

Secondly, the planet's population reached nearly eleven billion people in the second half of the 21st century, which was unsustainable for two reasons. Firstly the forests had been cut down and the land used for agriculture and living space, and secondly there was a shortage of food. Some countries had been attempting for many, many years, to reduce the rise in their populations by penalising people with more than two children, but at the same time the average age of people at death had risen from around seventy five years to ninety years. The planet could not sustain the population growth, and feed everyone.

The population growth was not, and is not, our concern here, but the yield of plants used for food is. Our main concern is to increase the yields of food plants, without the use of chemicals wherever possible. The work we have done here using cross breeding and genetics has increased the yield of most food plants by more than sixty percent, without the side effects experienced in the first attempts at genetically engineered food, which partly led to the near collapse of the world's ecosystems. Similar results have been achieved elsewhere in the field of animals bred for food. We do not work in that area. You'll see that later in your retraining.

Finally, it was known for a long time that nature provided plants that could be harvested and used for natural medicines. For years, pharmaceutical companies manufactured artificial medicines which, over the long term, proved to be dangerous to the health of humans when trace elements of the drugs were passed down between generations. We have spent a considerable amount of time, and expertise, analysing every type of plant occurring naturally on the planet, and have been reasonably successful in isolating the chemicals, or drugs, needed to treat most ailments. We still have a lot of work to do, but keep hoping for the big breakthrough that will eliminate the necessity for synthetic drugs. Viruses and bacteria have a habit of mutating when we least expect it.'

She paused again for a few moments.

'Do you have any questions?' she said.

'Yes,' Julia said. 'Do all the Complexes have similar research facilities?'

Ronaldo quickly glanced at Patricia, paused, and said. 'Yes. We share our results with the other Complexes, and they share theirs with us. Each Complex specialises in vegetation from it's designated part of the world. Here we specialise in European vegetation. There are also three research centres specialising in marine biology. They are also run by The Consortium, but are separate from the Complexes.'

'Is that because all of the Complexes are inland, in remote areas?'

'Yes. None of the Complexes are near the oceans. When they were built the oceans were considered to be too toxic to live near. The marine biology centres were built later.'

For some reason I thought he wasn't telling us the whole truth. I had no tangible reason not to believe him, but there was something in his manner…something he was holding back from us.

'How big is the Flora Centre?' I asked.

'The Flora Centre consists of two domes with a ground area of twenty five square kilometres each. One is used for food plants and the other for trees and medicinal vegetation,' Rose said, looking around. 'Are there any more questions?'

We looked around at each other. There was no response.

Trevor William Poate

'Alright. I'll show you around the food dome first. I'm sure that will be of most interest to you. You'll also have an opportunity to taste some fruit and vegetables for the first time.'

We followed her out of the room, and along a corridor into another room where there were black overalls hanging on the wall.

'You each need to put one of these on,' she said, taking one off a peg. 'They will protect you from the insects in the domes.'

'Insects?' Calista said.

'Yes. There are a lot of insects in the domes, particularly the tree dome. They are needed for pollination and to recycle dead material. You need to wear the overalls to avoid being bitten or stung by any of them.'

Each of us took one of the overalls and put it on, before following her into an air lock leading to the first dome. As we entered the dome, the first thing I noticed was the smell. It was sweet, unlike anything I'd ever smelled before.

'What is the smell?' I asked Rose.

'It's the smell of the flowers. Plants use the smell and colour of their flowers to attract insects which will pollinate them. That's why insects are so important in the natural world. As we walk around you'll see what I mean.'

The air in the dome was also quite cool on my face. For some reason I had expected it to be warm. I wasn't used to changes in temperature, because the Complex had been kept at a constant temperature throughout. I was glad I was wearing the overall.

The first section we saw contained plants displaying a myriad of coloured flowers. I think we were all stunned at the beauty and the diversity, because there were gasps as we moved from one group of plants to another, smelling the flowers and feeling the strange texture of the leaves and petals. I was surprised that some leaves were brown. I'd always thought that leaves were always green. Rose explained that the leaves on plants had a short life cycle, and that when they were dead they turned brown and fell off. She was constantly explaining about each type of plant, telling us their names and about their importance to the ecosystem. There were small, furry, brown and yellow insects flying around making a buzzing sound. She told us they were 'bees', and explained they were very important for pollinating the flowers. They were amazing.

After about an hour we were taken to a small open shuttle, and told to take a seat.

'The dome is too big for you to walk around it all, so we'll take you on a tour of the outer reaches on the shuttle,' Rose said. 'I want to show you the area where field crops are grown.'

The first fields we saw were about a fifteen minute ride away. Again, Rose explained what each crop was called, and it's use for food. There was a wheat field, a barley field, a maize field and another fifteen or twenty vegetable crops such as cabbages and potatoes. We'd all seen pictures of the plants, but seeing them grow in the fields was somehow peculiar.

'How many people work in the dome?' Julia asked.

'There are about a hundred and fifty people looking after the plants, and sixty five scientists and technicians working on the genetics and yields,' she told us.

'What happens to the food grown here?' Julia continued.

'Most of it is sent to the Centre where it is processed and forms the basis of your diet.'

'You mean our food is made from real plants?'

'Yes. But during the processing it loses all resemblance to it's natural state, and is combined with preservatives, vitamins and minerals, adjusted for each person's needs. Unfortunately the processing also removes the natural flavours and colours, so we colour and flavour your food to make it palatable.'

The shuttle continued along for another hour and a half, passing rows of fruit trees such as oranges and apples, and some low bushes, with small green berries called olives, before stopping at the first of rows of clear plastic buildings.

'This is where we grow some of the plants which prefer higher humidity and heat than the main dome can provide, such as tomatoes and grapes. They are called tunnels, which their shape suggests. I'll show you around one or two before we go for lunch, when you'll have your first taste of our produce.'

We followed her into the first tunnel. She explained that it was a nursery, where seedlings were propagated prior to being transplanted into other tunnels to mature. There were thousand of small plants packed together in a water bath.

'We use hydroponics to grow the plants,' she said. 'The plants are kept in temperature-controlled water baths and fed nutrients, processed from naturally rotted vegetation, to encourage growth. The system avoids the need for soil, which the other crops you've seen elsewhere grow in. They are also given chemical fertiliser to improve their yields and avoid infections. In the future we hope to eliminate all the chemicals we use. The plants here grow much more quickly than those outside and we can harvest them four or even five times a year. The tunnels are about twenty metres wide and sixty metres long.'

It was very warm and, for the first time in our lives, we sweated. We went into an adjacent tunnel full of tomato plants laden with fruit.

'We will harvest these in the next few days, and another crop will be brought in to mature,' she told us. 'We'll have a look in one other tunnel before we return to the training room.'

She led us into a tunnel five or six down the row, where the temperature was even higher and the variety of plants more diverse.

'We use this tunnel, and six others, for experimentation. We are constantly attempting to improve the yields of the plants and shorten the time they take to mature. We monitor every aspect of each plant's growth, and yield every day. The nutrients we use are adjusted according to the results. You can see one of the scientists taking some readings,' she said, pointing down the tunnel.

'How do the improved plants help the outside world?' Calista asked.

'When we are satisfied we have an improved strain, we try it out in one of the main tunnels for five growing cycles. If the improvements are satisfactory we send seeds outside where they are trialled for two seasons before being released for general use. The whole idea is to feed everyone using as little land as possible. The intention is to allow as much cultivated land as possible to return to it's natural state.'

'Do the Renegades benefit from your research?' Calista asked.

'The Renegades? Why do you ask about them?'

'I'm just curious about how they survive on their own.'

Rose looked at Patricia for guidance.

'You don't need to concern yourself with the Renegades,' Patricia said.

We looked around for a short while before heading back for lunch. We were taken to a room where there were plates full of some of the vegetables and fruits we had seen during the morning. We looked at each other, unsure what to do. We'd only ever used spoons before, but there were no spoons, just two other types of plastic implements.

'These are knives, and these are forks,' Rose said, as we picked them up and examined them. 'We use the knife to cut the food, like this,' she said, picking up a tomato and cutting it into four pieces, 'and then the fork to pick up each piece and put it into our mouth. You try it.'

Each of us picked up a tomato and copied what she had done. The knives were very sharp and the four prongs of the fork skewered the pieces very easily. There was laughter around the room at some of our attempts, but it soon stopped when we tentatively put the tomato pieces into our mouths and tasted natural food for the first time. I didn't know what to expect, and the consistency of the tomato came as a shock. It had a sweet flavour unlike anything I had tasted in the food we usually ate, was full of seeds, and had a liquid centre. The skin was smooth and chewy.

'Try one of these,' she said, picking up an onion and peeling it.

Each of us picked one up, peeled it as she had shown us, cut it, and put it into our mouths. It had a sharp taste, and Calista immediately spat it out. Rose laughed.

'I deliberately told you to try the onion to demonstrate the difference in flavours between the foods,' she said. 'As time goes on you'll get used to them all. I should explain, our tongues have receptors on the surface, which detect five different types of taste. They are sweetness; savouriness, bitterness, sourness and saltiness. All food tastes fall into one of those categories. There are also herbs and spices, which you haven't seen yet, but will use later on when you are taught to prepare your own food. I'll go through the rest of the items here with you and explain how to eat them.'

We were there for over two hours as we tried different things. Rose showed us how to peel oranges and explained about some parts of fruits not eaten, such as the cores of apples. I can't say any of us felt satisfied with our meal, but the mere fact we were eating real food for the first time compensated for our hunger.

When we'd finished she told us we would spend the afternoon in the other dome, viewing the trees and other vegetation. She took us to wash our hands, and led us to the entrance to the second dome, where we spent three hours on one of the open shuttles, touring around. She explained about the different types of trees, some of the undergrowth, and showed us fields of grasses and bushes. The plants were watered by a spray system, near the roof of the dome, which created artificial rain once a day. There were far more insects than in the first dome, some decorated with amazing colours, crawling or flying around. Photographs could never express the true beauty of what we saw. It was almost moving, in a way I'd never imagined I could experience.

'I can't wait to go outside and see more of this,' Calista said, during our ride.

'Neither can I. Can you imagine how much more there is. Rose said that this was a tiny fraction of the variety of plants around the world. It's amazing. I never imagined there were so many, and we haven't even seen any animals yet.'

It was around five o'clock when we arrived back at the training room. Patricia told us the shuttle was due at five thirty, and that we could spend the last half an hour asking questions. There were so many, that none of us knew where to start. We did ask a few, but the time soon came for us to leave. We all thanked Rose for her patience and understanding, and made our way to the shuttle for the ride back to the Quarantine Centre. During the return journey, Ronaldo told us we would be going to visit the Fauna Centre the next day.

We ate our usual food that evening, all of us talking excitedly about our day's excursion, rather like children with a new toy. Calista and I went to bed early, after gazing out at the moon and stars again, dreaming of the outside and talking about what we'd seen, and our trip the next day.

We had a shorter journey the following morning. It was still an early start, but we arrived at the Fauna Centre before eight o'clock, still feeling excited from the day before.

Patricia didn't accompany us, only Ronaldo. He explained that she disliked 'animal' food and felt uncomfortable with some of the things we were going to see. He also told us the visit would only last the morning, after which we could try some of the meat before returning to the Quarantine Centre during the afternoon.

We were met by a man called Toby. He showed us

to a training room where he explained the work they did. The Fauna Centre consisted of two areas. The first one was called the Animal Husbandry Unit, and the second The Processing Unit. There were no, what he called, exotic animals in the Centre. The Centre was only concerned with animals bred for food. Exotic, or wild, animals, were studied elsewhere. He explained that the purpose of animal husbandry was to cross-breed different strains of each type of animal to improve yields of meat, and milk from cows, which was mainly processed into 'cheese' and 'butter'. He explained what they were because we didn't know. They sounded horrible!

The area included laboratories where scientists analysed the results and suggested improvements to the cross breeding processes. The Processing Unit was concerned with developing methods of turning the raw meat into food suitable for humans. He also explained that most of the animal's natural feed came from the Flora Centre, and was added to chemical supplements developed by the scientists.

The talk lasted for about an hour. We all put on overalls, similar to the ones at the Flora Centre, and he led us to the Animal Husbandry Unit first, where he showed us around some of the breeding groups. He explained that they didn't keep large herds of animals, just sufficient for their breeding experiments. There were various breeds of each of the animals. He explained that the different breeds preferred different natural habitats, and that the scientists took that into account when they made their recommendations.

The animals in this, the European Complex, were cows, sheep, pigs, goats, and chickens. He told us that the other Complexes bred similar animals, but with a few changes because of regional preferences. For example, the Central and Southern African Complex also bred ostriches, which he told us were very large birds, as tall as a man. The Arab Complex didn't breed pigs, for religious reasons, but did breed camels, an animal able to survive in arid regions needing very little water.

'How many people work here?' Kevin asked.

'Sixty five. There are twenty scientists and ten breeding experts. The rest look after the animals' welfare.'

'What's the smell?' I asked.

'As you have seen, the animals defecate wherever they happen to be standing. The pungent smell in here comes from that. It needs to be cleaned up every day, and the animals hosed down with water to stop infections. The animals are inoculated against most diseases, but nature always seems to manage to develop new ones. Samples of their faeces are analysed by the scientists, but most of it is sent to the Flora Centre and used as fertiliser. Did Rose explain that to you yesterday?'

'No she didn't,' I said.

'Well, plants need nutrients to grow. All of the animals here are herbivores, so only eat plant matter. Once they have digested the nutrients they need, they defecate the waste which is returned to the Flora Centre where it is used to naturally feed the crops, some of which are returned here as feed for the animals. It's a natural cycle.'

'So the plants feed the animals, who feed the plants,' Calista said.

'Yes. That's right. If there are no more questions I'll show you around the Processing Unit and then you can try some meat.'

We followed him out of the Animal Husbandry Unit into another building which also smelled, but not as pungently.

'This is the Milking Unit,' he said opening a door where there were fifty or so cows standing, almost to attention, with hoses attached to their nipples, or udders. There were different breeds. Some were brown, some black and some black and white.

'The milk from these cows is collected twice a day. It is then pasteurised, which is essentially boiled, to kill any latent bacteria. It is then sent to the Processing Unit where it is turned into various dairy products, such as the butter and cheese I told you about earlier. There are hundreds of different types of cheese, each one tasting different according to the type of milk used, and the method of processing. Milk is also used for drinking and cooking.'

'What do you mean by type of milk?' Julia asked.

'The flavour of a cow's milk changes according to the feed and breed. The different flavours determine the type of cheese. There are other additives used, but that is the basic difference between cheeses. Goats milk is also sometimes used to make cheese.'

We left the Milking Unit and entered a very cold room where there were dozens of dead animals hanging up.

'This is the abattoir,' he said. 'When the animals have reached maturity, or their useful life finishes, such as when the milking cows stop lactating, they are brought here and slaughtered. Some are taken by the scientists for research, and the rest are processed for food. Unfortunately we are not slaughtering any animals today, so I can't show you the process.'

'Who eats the food from here?' I asked.

'There isn't very much. It's all consumed by people here and in the Quarantine Centre. The scientists will take DNA from each animal and, if the yield and quality has improved, the DNA will be used outside to clone more stock using other animals as hosts.'

'I read somewhere about chickens and eggs,' Kevin said.

'Yes. Like the other animals, the chickens are bred for meat, but also for laying eggs. A chicken can only produce one egg each day, so, the scientists concern themselves with the nutrients within the egg. Like the milking cows, the eggs are different according to the feed the chickens are given.'

'What do you do with the eggs?'

'Some are fertilised and become new chickens, the rest are used for food.'

'You mean you eat the eggs?' Calista said, pulling a face.

'Yes. You can try one later,' he said, chuckling. 'If you follow me, I'll quickly show you the Meat Processing Unit before we finish.'

We followed him into an adjacent room where there were a few men and women cutting the animals' carcases into small pieces.

'Each type of animal is processed differently,' he said. 'Pig's meat is often cured, or smoked, to give it a different flavour, while cow's meat, or beef as it is known, is usually cut into large pieces before being prepared to eat.'

'What happens to the skin and organs?' I asked.

'The skin, bone and organs are processed into feed for the animals. I know I told you they are herbivores, but they will eat the processed feed, particularly the pigs. Nothing is wasted. Historically the skin was used for clothing and people ate the organs, but we don't do that here. In some places on the outside people still do, but it's not very common.'

We followed him around for ten minutes before he said we needed to return to the training room. After removing our overalls we re-entered the room where plates full of grey and white 'stuff' were waiting for us.

'These are examples of how we eat meat,' he said.

'What's been done to it?' Julia asked.

'It's been cooked. We don't usually eat raw meat. You'll be shown how to cook meat during the next week or two, but in the meantime, try some.'

There was a label next to each plate. Cow (beef),

sheep (lamb), pig (pork and ham), and poultry (chicken). We took turns in tasting a piece from each plate. I liked it. Each one tasted different, especially the ham, and had a different texture.

'Usually meat is eaten accompanied by vegetables. There are many different ways of cooking the meat, each giving it a slightly different taste, and texture,' Ronaldo said. He'd been quiet most of the morning. 'I'll be showing you the different methods later this week. Patricia will concentrate on the vegetables and fruits. You have a lot to learn, and practice.'

'Do we have to eat meat?' Calista asked.

'No. Some people don't like it, or think it's wrong to eat animals. It's your choice. But, you should try more of it before deciding. The way I look at it is that all the domesticated animals we eat are herbivores. Therefore, meat is created from plants, so it's still plant food. In some places people do eat carnivorous animals, but it is rare.'

'Try an egg, Toby said to Calista. 'It's only been boiled and the shell removed, and won't hurt you.'

'What's the yellow bit in the middle?' she asked, picking up half an egg and looking at me.

'I don't know,' I said.

'It's called the yoke. It's what would have become the chicken if it had been fertilised. The white part is called the albumen. It's the protein used during the egg's development into a chicken,' Toby said.

Calista took a bite, as we all watched. 'It tastes strange. The yellow bit is dry, and the white bit is sort of…I don't know, strangely smooth.'

'Do you like it?' I asked.

'Yes. You try one.'

I picked one up and took a bite. 'It's alright,' I said, after a few moments.

The rest of the group also tried a piece. No one disliked it, but no one tried a second piece.

'Is there any cheese we can try?' Julia asked.

'You'll be able to try some at the Quarantine Centre,' Ronaldo said.

We tried the meats again, before he said it was time to go. On the shuttle, he told us the rest of the afternoon was free for us to do anything we wanted, but gave us the page number and access code of some reading he wanted us to do before meeting up the next morning.

'Do you think the Officers experiment with people in the same way they do with animals?' Calista asked, as we started reading.

'I don't know. Why would they?'

'But if they did?'

'What do you mean?'

'Well, Patricia said the other day that The Experiment had to be kept secret because people outside might think the Consortium was breeding a 'Super Race'. What if we are part of that 'Super Race'?'

'If we are, I can't imagine why they are letting us leave here.'

'We haven't left yet.'

'No. We haven't…'

We spent the afternoon and evening reading about different methods of preparing meat and vegetables for eating. There were pictures showing pots and pans, utensils and cooking machines, some of which we recognised as the strange equipment in our accommodation.

We made our way to the training room after breakfast the next morning.

'From now on you are going to be eating natural food, so you will need to learn quickly if you don't want to starve,' Patricia said, smiling. 'Over the next week I will teach you how to prepare and cook vegetables and fruit, and Ronaldo will teach you how to prepare and cook meat. I don't touch or eat meat because I don't like the taste or the feel of it. You can decide for yourselves whether you do, but to start with, I suggest you try it. By this time next week, we expect you to be able to prepare and cook your food without any assistance from us. There is a lot to learn, and it will take many months before you have tried the thousands of options available. But for now, we will teach you the basics to enable you to survive. The first thing you will learn is the names of the most commonly used vegetables, fruits, and meats, and the names of the implements used to prepare and cook them. I assume you all completed your reading yesterday?'

There was a murmur around the room.

'Good. I'll take that as a 'yes'. From now on there will be a short test at the end of each day. We need to gauge your progress, so we know when you need additional instruction.'

She paused, and briefly looked at Ronaldo, before saying. 'Open page F21a in your workbooks. The access code is P41c/1. Read the first page, and then we'll begin…'

Calista and I were hungry and tired by the end of each day. Patricia was true to her word. If we wanted to eat, we needed to learn how to prepare and cook our own food. To be fair, she did help, and so did Ronaldo, but we still felt hungry.

We had been given some pills to take each day. They told us they had been developed to help our digestive system become used to the change in diet. All of us felt a little ill for the first few days, but we soon started enjoying the results of our efforts once the pills took effect.

It was the versatility of the food that surprised us most. The myriad of textures, colours and tastes was beyond our wildest expectations. The raw food could be cooked in many different ways, and some eaten uncooked, but not understanding which foods accompanied each other, and how much to prepare, was confusing. Some of our early efforts were horrible! For example, we didn't understand that potatoes are not usually cooked with fruit, or why. But, the hardest thing was learning how long to cook things for, and at what temperature. A lot of food was inedible by the time we'd finished attempting to cook it, and by the end of the week we all had burn marks on our hands or arms from touching hot pots and pans, or the hot cookers.

Fabio and Tina became the most accomplished of us all. At times, it seemed to me that they had cooked before, because they seemed to understand what foods could be mixed together and rarely made a mistake. Perhaps they had read more than we had, but then again…

At the end of each day, Patricia conducted our test in a side room. It wasn't done as a group. Instead, she asked us questions as couples. Each test only lasted a few minutes, but I noticed Fabio and Tina's always seemed to take longer. I wondered what they were being asked that we weren't.

Chapter 7

Fertility

*O*n our next rest day we were given access to any foods we wanted, and told we would have to feed ourselves without supervision for the first time. Patricia came to see us late in the afternoon.

'Calista. You and the other women will have the operation to reverse your sterilisation tomorrow. Callum and the other men will have theirs the day after tomorrow.'

'Tomorrow?' Calista said, in surprise.

'Yes. The operation takes about an hour, and you will be first. A nurse will come for you at seven thirty. Be ready and don't have any breakfast. You will stay in the Medical Centre for a day or two before coming back here. We expect you to be fit enough to continue your training in about three or four days.'

'What do you do to me?'

'We reconnect your fallopian tubes. Do you know what they are?'

'Yes. Is that all?'

'Basically yes. But you will need to take some drugs to stimulate your egg production.'

'How long for?'

'Everyone is different. But you're young, so probably not very long.'

'Is the operation safe?'

'Yes. It's very uncommon for it to fail, so don't worry.'

'When could I get pregnant?'

'You'll be on drugs until you finish here, so not before then.'

'When will I be able to see her?' I asked.

'Tomorrow evening.'

'And how long does my operation take?'

'About an hour as well. You will be sore for a while,' she said, glancing at my crotch and smiling, 'but should be fully fit again within a few days!'

'What do you do to me?'

'We reconnect your testes to your prostate. Do you know what they are?'

'Yes, I do. Is that all?'

'Yes. I must go now, I need to talk with the others.'

'What will I do tomorrow?'

'We have a project for you to do. Ronaldo will tell you about it in the morning. You can also practice your cooking, if you want to. Be at the training room at eight o'clock.'

'Alright.'

She left us staring at each other, deep in thought…

The nurse came for Calista the following morning and took her to the Medical Centre. I wasn't allowed to go with her, so waited for a few minutes before making my way to the training room. Ronaldo was already there, but no one else.

'The others should be here in a few minutes,' he said, looking at the clock on the wall. 'How's Calista?'

'Nervous. The operation this morning came as a surprise. We knew it was going to be done, but thought we'd have a few days notice.'

'We deliberately spring it on you because we don't want to give you too much time to worry about it. She'll be alright, and so will you tomorrow.'

The others were arriving. He briefly spoke with each of them before gesturing for us to sit down.

'As you know, most of this week will be taken up recovering from your operations. However, that doesn't mean you have nothing else to do. The four of you can spend today practicing your cooking, or you can start the project we want you to do before the end of the week, while you're resting. We will provide food for you while you are recovering.'

He paused for a few moments before continuing. 'We want you to prepare a one hour presentation, using your workbooks, to be given later this week. We'd like to know what you like or dislike about the Complex, what you feel could be improved, your perceptions about how it is managed, and anything else you think we should know. We'd also like to know what you understand by 'democracy'.'

'Who will we give the presentation to?' Kevin asked.

'We'll connect your workbooks to the screen behind me, and you will give it to the group, Patricia, and me,' he said, glancing at the screen on the wall behind him.

'How do we prepare the presentation?' I asked.

'There's a program on your workbook which I'll show you how to use. It's very easy.'

'Where do we get our information from?'

'I'll give you the page numbers and access codes for all the relevant information you might need, but we are really interested in your thoughts about the Complex. We are looking for ways we can improve it. For example, you may feel there should be more interaction with other people, apart from on the Community Days, or you may think the Officers should be more accessible. You can tell us anything you want to, but remember, the Complex is a closed community, so any suggestions must take that into account.'

'Will the women do the same thing?'

'No, we have a different project for them.'

He looked at each of us in turn, then said. 'Now, do you want to practice your cooking this morning, or start on the project?'

We glanced at each other, and Kevin said, 'I'd like to find out more about using herbs and spices. Can I do that?'

'Yes, you can. Anyone else?'

We all nodded. It seemed like a good idea.

'Alright. We'll do that this morning and then I'll show you the presentation program this afternoon, and you can start the project.'

We had an interesting morning trying different herbs and spices, and learning which ones complemented different foods. Some of them were very pungent, such as garlic, and others very hot, such as chilli, which burned our tongues, and in my case nearly suffocated me when I bit off too much and nearly choked as my throat constricted. I needed a lot of water before I could breath properly again. Ronaldo just laughed at my discomfort, and said it was a warning not to try anything without taking his advice first!

After lunch, he showed us how to use the presentation program and gave us access to the information we could use. By five o'clock we'd finished for the day, and I made my way to the Medical Centre to see Calista. She was awake when I was shown into the room where she was lying in bed. I assumed the other women were in similar rooms on their own.

'How are you feeling?' I asked her, sitting down next to the bed and giving her a kiss on her forehead.

'Sore, and tired,' she replied, smiling, 'but it'll be worth it if we can have children.'

'It's my turn tomorrow, so I expect I'll be sore as well,' I said, remembering what Patricia had told us the previous evening.

I told her about my morning's cooking, and the project. She made a few suggestions for things I could include in my presentation, but I could tell she was tired, and after an hour I left, made my way to our accommodation, and started preparing my dinner.

I'd arranged to meet the others in the recreation room later that evening for a chat about the project. We talked about our ideas for improvements to the Complex and what Ronaldo meant by democracy. Fabio seemed to know a lot about it, which surprised me. He told us he had studied different ones in his spare time. Something seemed odd about what he said, but I couldn't put my finger on what it was until he mentioned the Renegades. He'd never mentioned them before. I asked him what he knew about them, but he became defensive, saying he only knew what we'd all been told by Patricia and Ronaldo. I didn't believe him, but didn't press him to tell us more.

By nine o'clock we'd run out of things to say and I went back to my accommodation, and an early night in bed, on my own. When I passed Fabio's accommodation I could have sworn I heard him talking to Tina, which seemed strange, because she too should have been in a recovery room, but maybe I was mistaken…

My operation was due at nine o'clock the next morning and I planned to call in to see Calista beforehand. The nurse told me they expected her to be back at the accommodation in the afternoon, and so would I.

'Don't I have to stay here overnight?'

'No. Both of you will rest tomorrow and be back training the day after. A doctor will call in to see you both tomorrow and check on your progress. The operation is done using a method called micro-surgery, so you won't even notice a scar.'

Calista and I chatted for a few minutes before I left for my operation. 'I'll see you later,' I said, nervously.

She was lying on the bed, using her workbook, when I returned to our accommodation.

'How are you feeling?' she asked, as I gingerly walked over to her.

'Alright. Patricia was right, I do feel a little sore, but not as much as I had expected.'

'Good. I feel a lot better than I expected to.'

'What are you doing?' I said, joining her on the bed.

'Patricia gave us a project to do, but not the same as yours.'

'What is it?'

'We have to give a presentation on the different roles of men and women in society, both historically, and now.'

'That sounds interesting.'

'It's a strange subject. I mean, apart from carrying babies, the roles are interchangeable. There's almost nothing I can think of that both men and women can't do.'

'Now, yes, but years ago women looked after the

children and the home, while men went out to work, or caught the food if you go back far enough. You know, hunter gatherers,' I said, smiling.

'I know, but what relevance is that to us?'

'Perhaps there are differences outside.'

'Do you think so?'

'I don't know. I suppose we'll find out when we go to the Rehabilitation Centre.'

'When do we go there?'

'In about ten days, I think.'

'I wonder what we'll do between now and then.'

'More cooking, and our projects, I suppose.'

'We haven't been told about work or living outside.'

'Maybe that's what we'll do.'

'Maybe…'

Chapter 8

Contributing

*W*e gave our presentations two days later. They raised some interesting questions, which we discussed at length with Patricia and Ronaldo, who didn't appear in the least surprised by anything we said. I suppose they had heard it all before from other people they had retrained.

On reflection they didn't tell us anything, just listened and took notes on their workbooks. Calista asked about the relevance of their project, but they cleverly deflected the question.

'Tomorrow we will tell you about the various main religious groups around the world, and during the last week of your time here, we will tell you about your living and work arrangements outside. You will get more information in the Rehabilitation Centre, but we need you to have a grounding in life outside before you leave here.'

'When will we leave here?' Julia asked.

'In eight days time,' Ronaldo said.

'That's all for today, we'll start again at eight o'clock in the morning.' Patricia said, as she prepared to leave the room.

'Can we do any reading before tomorrow?' I

asked.

'No. We'll tell you everything you need to know in the morning. You have a few hours left this afternoon, so I want you, Kevin and Julia, to cook a meal for everyone this evening. Callum and Calista, it will be your turn tomorrow, Liam and Abigail, your turn the next day, and lastly, Tina and Fabio the day after. We'll join you for the meal this evening,' she said, addressing each of us in turn, before glancing at Ronaldo.

We looked at each other, and smiled.

'I'm glad you're first,' I said to Julia.

'Thanks…' she replied, looking at Kevin.

The meal went very well. Remembering that Patricia was a vegetarian, Kevin and Julia made vegetable soup, followed by spicy rice with vegetables, and fresh fruit for desert. I was very impressed with their efforts. Patricia told us she wouldn't join us for our meals during the rest of the week, so that we could cook meat if we wanted to, but Ronaldo would.

We all met at eight o'clock the following morning. Ronaldo and Patricia shared the day's training, explaining to us the history of the major religions still practiced around the world.

The concept of religious belief was something we hadn't experienced. We found it hard to understand why people would live their lives according to a set of rules laid down hundreds of years ago, advocating some sort of all-seeing, intangible, 'God', overseeing their lives. Patricia suggested it was how, in ancient times, people used the concept of a God to explain events they didn't understand, such as an earthquake, but regular praying, or worshiping an invisible God didn't make sense to any of us. Some religions even worshipped animals!

I could understand how people living by a set of rules laid down in books by the wise men of their day might be attractive, but that was all. After all, we lived by rules laid down by the Officers.

The strangest thing to grasp was why people believing in one religion hated people believing in another, to the point where they would go to war over their beliefs. I thought back to what Karl had told us about The Middle East War being caused by religious hatred, and how millions of people had died.

The essentials of each religion were very similar. There was a God, or series of Gods, whose rules were communicated to people by prophets of one sort or another, usually in the form of a written text. If people wanted to go to 'Heaven', somewhere where they would meet their God when they died, they should study the texts and abide by the rules. However, there was no evidence that 'Heaven' existed, or that after we died our 'Spirit' went anywhere.

Interestingly, in some religions, women were subservient to men, which explained why Calista and the other women in our group, had been given their project to do. Our project came in useful as well. Ronaldo explained that in many places the religious leaders acted as a quasi-government, deciding the rules under which people lived, based on their own interpretation of the historical texts. The leaders were usually men, and needed to have an understanding of how their communities inter-related.

Patricia explained that during the mid 21st century, governments throughout the world tried to reconcile the supporters of each religion, and eventually in 2057 most religious groups came to an agreement to live peacefully together. There had still been some minor skirmishes, but nothing as serious as the one in 2029 when Iran attacked Israel for the last time.

She explained that we would meet religious people, and would be living in areas where religion was practiced, which was why we needed to know about them. She advised us not to question the beliefs of those people, just to accept them. She even suggested that some of us might join in the practice, which seemed unlikely.

'Tell us about the Renegades,' Calista said.

'You asked about them in the Flora Centre. What is so interesting about them?' Patricia said.

'I'm curious about them, that's all. Where do they live, and how?'

Patricia looked at Ronaldo, for what appeared to be confirmation she could talk about them. He nodded.

'The Renegades live outside, by which I mean outside of controlled society,' she said.

'Controlled? What does that mean?'

'Outside of…accepted society.'

'I'm confused,' Calista said. 'Accepted by who?'

'Accepted by the rest of the world.'

'And controlled by?'

'Controlled by...by the Regional Governments,' Patricia said hesitantly, glancing at Ronaldo again.

'Do you mean they don't conform, and don't do what they are told?'

'In a way, yes,' Ronaldo said, before Patricia could reply.

'So, where do they live?' I asked, trying to help out Calista, who looked at me and smiled.

'Mainly on islands.'

'Islands?'

'Yes. There are thousands of islands around the world. Some are uncontrolled, which is where they live.'

'Are they a problem?' I asked.

'Not really. They keep to themselves, and don't generally bother anyone else.'

'Are they religious?' Kevin said, getting back to the subject.

'Some are.'

'And the others?'

Patricia looked at Ronaldo again, and said. 'Most of the Renegade groups have been isolated for a long time, and have inter-bred, reducing their gene pool. They are... sometimes deformed, and susceptible to diseases eradicated in the... the civilised world and, yes, some are religious.'

'Civilised? Do you mean the 'controlled' world?'

'Yes, I suppose I do.'

'And deformed? What sort of deformities?' Julia asked.

'They have reduced intelligence and some physical deformities.'

'Such as?'

'You don't need to know...you are very unlikely to meet any of them.'

'How do people become Renegades?' Calista asked.

Ronaldo looked at Patricia again. They were clearly uncomfortable with the question. 'Occasionally people are rejected from society, and others choose to join them. A few are sent there for their own good,' Ronaldo said.

'What do you mean by, 'for their own good'?'

'Some people need help they can't get elsewhere.'

'I don't understand.'

'You don't need to.'

We'd exhausted the questions Patricia and Ronaldo were prepared to answer, and went back to our accommodation to cook our meal for the group. Most of us were becoming quite good cooks by that time, and I certainly enjoyed the challenge of cooking something new, even when it sometimes turned out wrong, despite following one of the recipes we'd been given! However, we didn't go hungry.

'Why do you think they are reluctant to tell us about the Renegades?' Calista asked, as we started cooking.

'I don't know, but they seem…almost scared of them, as though they are some kind of threat,' I replied.

'But, how can they be a threat? They're isolated, with almost no contact with anyone else.'

'Perhaps they have more contact than we are being told about.'

'Do you think so?'

'I think we should find out.'

The week's training in outside work practices covered aspects of personal interaction with colleagues, how working day to day with people was different from the isolated working we'd been used to, and the importance of discussing issues with people working with us. Having someone supervise our daily work was something we weren't used to, and the possibility of being reprimanded for bad work or not achieving our targets, were things we'd never experienced since being children at school. In the Complex we just completed the day's tasks and started again the next day. If we had any problems we had an advisor we could contact by computer. None of us had ever worked outside of our own Multiplex, and having to leave our accommodation and go somewhere else to work with other people seemed strange.

'What sort of work will we be doing?' Julia asked Patricia one afternoon.

'It'll be very similar to your work here. In your case you will work in a hospital, and Kevin will work as a teacher.'

'Will we work and live with other people who have left the Complex?' I asked.

'No. You will be integrated into an existing community. People living near you will be told you have transferred from another region, and you must not tell them that you were in a Complex, or anything about it.'

There were murmurs around the room.

'That is very important,' Patricia continued, emphasising the word 'very'.

We had seen the holographic showing us pictures of the type of accommodation we would live in, so already knew what to expect, but we hadn't been told about things such as keeping it clean, or looking after the small garden surrounding it. Ronaldo explained that, although the accommodation was provided free, we were responsible for keeping it in good condition. He also explained we would find out more in the Rehabilitation Centre.

'Does everyone have the same type of accommodation?' I asked.

'No. There are different styles in different places, and the size and facilities vary according to your grade,' he said. 'The accommodation you will get will be very similar to those we've shown you, but I can't tell you exactly what it will look like. You'll find that out when you get there.'

'Where will we be living?' Kevin asked.

'I can't tell you that either.'

'Why not?'

Trevor William Poate

'Because I don't know!'

'Will it be near where we work?'

'Yes. It's usually within walking distance.'

'The holographic we saw showed furniture very different from the furniture here. Do we get to choose our own furniture?' Calista asked.

'You'll find out more about that at the Rehabilitation Centre, but yes you will. The accommodation allocated to you will be empty, and you will be given sufficient credits to buy whatever you need,' Patricia said.

By the end of the week we knew as much as we were likely to learn without actually going outside. The last day was left for us to pack our few belongings, and rest. Ronaldo told us that we would leave the Quarantine Centre the next morning, and that the journey would take most of the day.

The Dancing Dolls

Trevor William Poate

Part Two

Outward Bound

Trevor William Poate

The Dancing Dolls

Trevor William Poate

Chapter 1

Relocation

*T*he eight of us met Patricia in the training room at nine o'clock the next morning.

'You have to go now,' she said. 'There's a shuttle waiting for you. I won't be going with you, but you will be accompanied by two security officers as far as the Rehabilitation Centre, where you'll be met by new trainers.'

She took us to the shuttle and wished us well before we left. Ronaldo was also there, and we thanked him for his help.

'What will you do now?' I asked Patricia.

She looked at Ronaldo, and said. 'We have a few more weeks here, before a weeks leave.'

'Both of you?' I said.

'Yes. Didn't you know? Ronaldo and I are married, or coupled, as you call it. We spend part of our time here, and part in the Rehabilitation Centre where you are going, with breaks in between.'

'No. I didn't know you are coupled,' I said, as I looked at them both in amazement. They had never shown any affection in our company, or given any other indication they were coupled.

'You should get on the shuttle now,' Ronaldo said. 'Best of luck. Follow your instincts and you'll be alright.'

'Yes, thanks. Goodbye.'

I thought it was a strange thing for Ronaldo to say. Luck had never featured in our lives, and I couldn't imagine what he meant by 'follow your instincts'.

Orderlies had taken our personal items, which we'd packed in plastic containers the day before, and loaded them onto the shuttle. It was different from those we'd been in before. It had windows! The journey started in a tunnel, but we soon emerged outside, and could see the landscape. After a while, bush like vegetation started appearing, and by the time we'd travelled for two hours we saw our first natural trees outside of the Fauna Centre.

'How much further do we have to go?' I asked one of the security men.

'The journey will take another four and a half hours,' he replied.

'How fast are we going?'

'Three hundred kilometres an hour. This is one of the high speed shuttles.'

I did a quick calculation in my head, and said to Calista. 'That means we'll have travelled nearly two thousand kilometres.'

'Where is the Rehabilitation Centre,' I said to the security man.

'It's on an island in the Atlantic Ocean. Tomorrow

you will be taken to it by boat.'

'Boat!' I said.

'Yes. The island is about a hundred and fifty kilometres from the African coast.'

'Have you been there?'

'No, I haven't.'

'I thought the Renegades lived on islands,' Calista said, glancing at me.

'I don't know anything about the Renegades,' he said, looking out of a window. He seemed uncomfortable with the question. I glanced at Fabio to see if he had reacted to the question, but didn't notice any change in his expression, though he did glance at Tina.

'Will you accompany us to the island?'

'No. We'll be met by two trainers at the coast. They will take you tomorrow, and we'll return here.'

We chatted among ourselves for the rest of the journey, commenting on the changing landscape, and speculating on the boat journey and the Rehabilitation Centre. Of course, none of us had ever seen the sea, or been in a boat, and there was an underlying excitement as our journey approached it's ending, in the first town we'd ever been to.

It was late afternoon when the shuttle slowed down and we started seeing buildings alongside the track. We saw our first people. They were dark brown. We'd never seen coloured people before, and stared at them as they went about their business. The biggest surprise was their clothing. It hadn't crossed our minds that they would be wearing different clothes from us. Our white one piece airspec suits seemed strange compared with the bright clothing they were wearing. The holographic we'd seen only showed people's heads, not their clothes.

One of the security men saw us staring at the clothes, and said. 'You'll be given new clothes in the morning, before you leave for the island.'

'What will they be like?' Abigail asked him.

'You'll be given a choice, but similar to those the people outside are wearing.'

The shuttle entered a tunnel and came to a stop a few minutes later. The door slid open to reveal a platform where a man and a woman were waiting for us. They introduced themselves as Robert and Mary. They were dressed in similar clothing to the people we had seen from the shuttle, but a little smarter. They said they were from the Rehabilitation Centre and would take us to the accommodation, where we would stay overnight, before continuing to the island the next morning. A group of dark skinned men collected our belongings from the shuttle and we made our way along the platform to a door, which opened into a corridor leading to a large white room, furnished with armchairs and tables.

'You'll stay here tonight. There's a dining room over there,' Robert said, pointing to a door, and then to a corridor, 'and your bedrooms are along there. You can relax here for the rest of the day or go to your rooms, and dinner will be ready at six o'clock.'

'What is the name of this town?' Kevin asked.

Trevor William Poate

134

'El Quatia,' Robert replied.

'Do you all still have your workbooks?' Mary asked, interrupting him.

We nodded that we did, and she said. 'Good. If you access page RH46 using the code DAY1, you can read up about the Rehabilitation Centre before we leave tomorrow. Do you have any questions?'

We glanced at each other, before shaking our heads in the negative.

'In that case we'll leave you now, and see you at dinner.'

Our belongings had been taken to our rooms and, having worked out which was ours, Calista and I had a quick look around the spartan bedroom and bathroom. The only thing of note about them was the absence of windows, unlike the Quarantine Centre. The lack of windows reminded us of our Multiplex, but we'd become used to windows in the Quarantine Centre, and felt claustrophobic. We opened our workbooks and started reading.

The island we were going to was called Graciosa. A causeway connected it to a larger island called Lanzarote, which was where we would spend time learning about living and working with other people. Graciosa had one small community, but Lanzarote was much bigger. It had towns with shops, buildings where people worked, and places used for entertainment. Our reading didn't explain what sort of entertainment, and we couldn't imagine what it might be, apart from a holographic cinema. The workbook also showed us maps of the two islands, and gave brief details of their history.

Although the people could speak our language, English, their natural language was Spanish. The workbook explained that we would learn a few words of Spanish, but that most of our interaction with people would be in English.

Before going to dinner, I asked Calista if she had noticed Fabio and Tina's reaction to our questions about the Renegades. She had noticed, and like me wondered who they really were. They behaved like us most of the time, but there was something different; something we couldn't put a finger on.

Dinner with Robert and Mary consisted of food local to the region. Mary told us it was called a Tagine, and was made from prawns, a type of seafood, and vegetables cooked in a spicy, watery, sauce. We'd never eaten any seafood before, although Ronaldo had told us about it at the Quarantine Centre. They showed us an uncooked prawn in it's shell. It was grey before being cooked, when it changed colour to an orangey pink. The meat was removed from the thin transparent skin, and then added to the vegetables before serving. They explained that we would be eating a lot of seafood during our stay, because it was a staple food on the islands.

They seemed friendly and answered our questions openly and, we thought, honestly, before telling us we would meet for breakfast at eight o'clock the next morning. After dinner we went back to our rooms and continued our reading.

After breakfast, Mary told us we would change our clothes for outside clothes. She took the women, and Robert took the men, to separate rooms where there was an array of clothing, similar to theirs, for us to choose from. We had no idea what we should choose, but Mary and Robert advised us, and showed us how to put them on. Our airspec suits had been simple one-piece garments, but our new clothes consisted of under clothing and brightly coloured over clothing held together with fastenings called zips, and buttons, which were fiddly to use. We laughed at our efforts, and eventually re-emerged into the lounge area looking very strange, at least to each other. Mary told us that when we reached the Rehabilitation Centre we would be taken to a shop to buy more clothing, and that it was usual to wear something different each day.

'We should go now,' Robert said, after we'd admired each other's clothes, 'the boat is waiting for us. We've had your belongings loaded already, so you just need to collect your workbooks and day bags.'

'How far away is the boat?' Liam asked.

'A few minutes walk,' Robert replied.

'Outside?'

'Yes.'

We were silent for a few moments. We were going outside for the first time, and I could feel my heart starting to beat faster with anticipation. We collected our day bags and workbooks, and returned to the lounge. I was holding

Calista's hand and could feel the sweat on her palm, as we followed Mary and Robert along a corridor, through a door, and outside.

The warmth was surprising as we took our first steps and breathed our first fresh air. I had to screw up my eyes at the uncomfortable intensity of the sun. There was a strange, almost salty, smell in the air, and there was a breeze. People were busy carrying boxes and bags full of…I don't know what. Calista squeezed my hand as we made our way along the concrete quay. We stopped at a gateway, and Robert spoke to a man who waved us past. A few metres further along there was a blue painted boat, about twenty five metres long, which had what looked like rooms on two levels. It had 'Atlantic Graciosa' painted in white on the side. I assumed that was it's name. I knew boats had names, but had no idea why. Numbers would have done! Robert stopped, spoke to another man, and gestured for us to follow him along a ramp leading up to the boat.

'What is that smell?' I asked Mary.

'Fish,' she said, pointing to some plastic boxes containing slippery looking, grey coloured, smelly, fish.

I looked along the quay. There were six or seven other boats being unloaded by strong, brown men.

'Most of these boats go out early, and then return with their catch of fish to sell in the local shops,' she continued.

We boarded the boat, and followed her into a room where there were chairs and tables fixed to the metal floor.

Trevor William Poate

138

'You should stay here until we leave the harbour,' Robert said. 'You can look around the boat once we are at sea.'

There were a few men moving around the boat, carrying boxes, and looking busy. We sat quietly, watching them going about their business. Suddenly the floor started vibrating and a rumbling sound came from somewhere below us. We jumped a little, wondering what was happening. We could see men untying ropes from the front and the back of the boat, before clambering onto the deck. A few moments later, the noise and vibration increased. Mary could see we were a little frightened, and explained that it was from the engine which powered the boat. She told us they had chartered the boat from Graciosa, where it was used for fishing, and that it was very old.

Slowly the boat eased away from the dock. Robert told us to wait where we were, and left the room. Mary waited with us, looking at each of us in turn, and smiling.

A few minutes later he returned, stood in front of us and said. 'The captain says the weather is good, so the journey should be calm. I know you have never been in a boat, so I have to explain a few things. Firstly, you need to wear one of these.' He picked up an orange jacket and put it on. 'It's a life jacket. If by any chance you fall off the boat, it will keep you afloat in the water. Secondly, once we leave the harbour the boat will start rocking from side to side and front to back. The movement is caused by waves and the boat making headway through the sea.

When you try and walk, you'll find it strange that the floor keeps moving beneath you. You'll get used to it, but try and hold on to something at first. Finally, the crew will serve some food in about three hours. Oh, I nearly forgot. Some of you may feel sick from the rocking motion. Don't worry, it's normal. If you do want to be sick, use one of the bathrooms, or lean over the side of the boat and make sure you face the back! Are there any questions?'

'How long is the journey?' Abigail asked.

'The captain thinks we should be there late this afternoon.'

'How will you know if any of us fall off the boat?' Kevin asked. He looked uncomfortable at the whole idea of going to sea.

'As soon as you hit the water an alarm will sound here on the boat. It's set off when your life jacket gets wet. Are there any more questions?'

No one else had any questions, so Robert handed each of us a life jacket, and showed us how to put it on.

'Alright. If you want to have a look around the boat you can. We're just leaving the harbour,' he said, glancing out of a nearby window. 'There are some restricted areas, but you're welcome to look around the rest.'

He sat down next to Mary and started quietly chatting to her.

The rest of us made our way out of the room onto a gangway at the side of the boat. Holding on to the railings, we gingerly walked towards the rear, where there was an open area with a few plastic seats the crew had put out for our use. The boat had already started rolling a little as the coast began to recede into the distance. The cool air blew our hair about, and the strength of the sun seemed to be less intense than when we were in the harbour. I guessed it was an illusion brought about by the breeze. There wasn't much to see on the boat, and after ten or fifteen minutes we returned to the rear and sat down. There were a lot of birds in the sky following us, and one or two other boats we could see nearby. We sat for a while, gazing at the birds, the water, and the waves. The sea seemed huge and blue, and the slightly lighter blue of the sky blending into it, indicated the horizon.

'I wonder what those boats are doing.' Calista said, pointing to them.

'Fishing, I imagine,' I said. 'How are you feeling?'

'Alright, so far.'

We ate, lunch, grilled fish with salad, soon after midday. It was hilarious! The fish still had it's skeleton, head, and tail, when the cook served us. Robert showed us how to remove the meat. It tasted oily, what little of it we managed to get off the small rubbery bones. Kevin was the only one of us who was sick and didn't each lunch, but I have to admit I nearly succumbed to the rolling of the boat a few times.

It was late in the afternoon when Robert pointed out an island appearing on the horizon.

'That's Lanzarote,' he said. 'We'll pass around the north of the island and dock at Graciosa in about an hour from now. The Rehabilitation Centre is only a short journey from the port, so we should be there in about one and half to two hours.'

The port was called Caleta del Sebo. There were a few small, brightly painted boats, tied up at the pier as we slowly manoeuvred alongside. A few men tied our boat to the pier, and scrambled aboard when it was secure.

Another man, with brown skin and dirty smelly clothes, attached a plank with railings to the side of the boat, and told us to walk along it. We made our way onto the wooden pier and walked to the shore, where there was a shuttle platform. Some men brought our belongings from the boat and, when Robert and Mary joined us, we sat waiting for a shuttle to arrive. About ten minutes later, an open-air shuttle with a cloth canopy stopped at the platform, and we got on after loading our luggage. The shuttle started and we passed by the houses of the small town and some open fronted shops where people were sitting, lazily taking the sun, and drinking a yellow liquid I couldn't identify. None of them took any notice of us, which I thought strange. I wondered what they thought the Rehabilitation Centre was and where we had come from.

The journey to the Centre took about fifteen minutes. When we arrived there were six brown men waiting to help us take our belongings to our new accommodation. They weren't as dark as the men we had seen at El Quatia, and their features were similar to ours.

Our adventure was beginning.

Trevor William Poate

Chapter 2

Rehabilitation

*E*ach couple had been allocated a small house, built in the style of the houses we'd seen elsewhere on the island, consisting of a living room, a bedroom, a bathroom and a kitchen. They were built from stone, with a cement covering painted white, and a flat roof that was reached by an outside staircase. The roof had tables and chairs where we could sit and eat our meals, and an array of photoelectric cells producing electricity.

There were a lot of insects crawling around the buildings, particularly small ones called 'ants', which Mary told us, at dinner that evening, would bite us if they crawled on our skins. Later, during the night, we were surprised at the noise some insects made. One insect, called a 'cricket', made a high pitched sound by rubbing it's hind legs together. I couldn't imagine why it did it, but it must have had a reason!

The rest of the Rehabilitation Centre was similarly built, the main building being in the middle, with the houses in a circle around it. I counted twelve houses in total. Six were occupied, four by us and two by, I assumed, Mary and Robert.

The areas between the buildings had pathways made of stone, with a short grass growing between them. The grass was mostly green, but in some areas, it was brown. Robert told us it had been scorched by the intense sunshine. There were also some trees with fruit growing. We knew what the fruit was from our lessons in the Quarantine Centre, but seeing the oranges, lemons, and other fruits hanging from the branches in the open air was new to us. There had been some fruit on the trees in the Flora Centre when we were there, but they seemed different and amazing, when we saw them outside. Many things would amaze us during our first few days.

We met up with Robert for breakfast in the main building where we had eaten the previous evening. It consisted of fresh fruit and bread, with butter spread over it. There was also something called 'jam', made from fruit, which was very sticky and sweet, and eaten with the bread and butter.

After breakfast, he told us we would spend our first morning choosing our new clothing in shops on Lanzarote, and the afternoon buying food. He gave each of us an identity card showing our name, our new registration number, and our photograph. He explained we would need it for our purchases, and later, access to our work places, and that we should be careful not to lose it. It doubled as a payment card. He told us the cards had 5,000 credits available, which should be enough for everything we would need while we were there. He explained, to buy things, we presented the card to the shopkeeper who used a computer to register the amount spent. Each computer was linked to a central system monitoring the amount of credits everyone had available. It was impossible to spend more than we had. Everyone was given their credit allowance once a month, according to their grade.

Patricia had told us about the financial and economic system used around the world. At one time it had been referred to as 'Communism', but was now called 'Federalism'. Essentially, every possible form of employment was graded, and each person received credits according to their grade. It had the advantage that everyone knew everyone else's credit allowance, and removed what she called inflation, a situation where the cost of things increased over time. It crossed my mind that there was no incentive for anyone to work harder, or for longer, than absolutely necessary. Her riposte had been that no one needed to anyway, because everyone had work and received credits sufficient for their needs, as long as they met their targets. People could, however, move from one job to another, and improve their grade as they became more skilled or experienced. She didn't explain how the Renegades paid for things, despite Calista's questions.

Towards the end of Robert's instruction, Mary arrived with two other people. She introduced them as Pablo and Susan and told us they would assist in our training. She explained that one of the four of them would accompany each of our couples during the day to help us with our shopping. Initially we would go together, and later as couples with one of them.

'Don't the locals think it strange we don't know about shopping and clothes and…things?' Julia said.

'They think you are from another region, learning about their customs, and doing some training. They are used to seeing people from here and have long ago stopped being curious,' Mary said.

After a few more instructions, Robert told us to go to our houses to collect our day bags, and meet back at the main building as soon as possible.

The shuttle stop was a short walk from the Centre, along a windy stone path. Mary told us the shuttle arrived eight times a day at fixed times, and that we should make sure we didn't miss it. It ran from a town called Orzola on Lanzarote, crossed the causeway, and did a loop around Graciosa before returning to Orzola. We would be using it every day when we started our work training.

We were on the platform a few minutes before it was due. Pablo explained the local shuttles were free, and that the long distance ones needed to be paid for from our credits, but that we wouldn't often need to use them because we would rarely leave the towns we would be living in.

The shuttle arrived with a few people already on it. After we found some seats, it left the platform and made its way around the small island, through Caleta del Sebo, past the harbour where we'd arrived the day before, stopping on three occasions for people to board or leave, then crossed the causeway before arriving in Orzola, about half an hour after we'd boarded. The landscape was very flat, with mainly small bushes and low trees. Almost everywhere was in sight of the sea. Pablo gave us a running commentary on what we were seeing, and on one occasion pointed out some cows grazing in a field.

I noticed that most people were wearing hats to protect themselves from the strong sunshine, which was only tempered by the breeze when the shuttle was moving. I asked Pablo where we could buy hats, and he said it would be one of our first purchases, which was just as well, because our skins were very pale from the years spent in the Complex and, in the case of Calista, was rapidly turning a bright pink colour. Everyone we'd seen since arriving had a naturally light-brown coloured skin, darkened further by the sun. No one was pink!

There were two covered platforms at Orzola. People were bustling around, some carrying luggage as they hurried towards their shuttles, others carrying plastic boxes or pushing trolleys. I felt uncomfortable, and lost, as I held Calista's hand and we followed Pablo and the others towards the exit, avoiding bumping into the busy, noisy, people.

We walked for a short distance into the centre of the town, and entered a large shop selling clothes. As we entered the shop Mary said she and Susan would help Calista and the other women select some clothes, while Robert and Pablo would go with the men. The selection was amazing. They helped us pick about a dozen sets of clothes, including some suitable for work. Robert explained that there were no formal types of work clothes, but there were loose rules about what we should or shouldn't wear. What he called 'casual' clothes were acceptable around the Rehabilitation Centre and the town, but for work we needed to be, what he called, 'smart'. I didn't fully understand the difference, but took his word for it. Each item of clothing had a tag attached, displaying the price in credits. We had so many bags of clothes by the time we'd finished, that he arranged for them to be sent to the shuttle station for us to collect on our way back to the Centre. The only things we kept with us were the hats we'd bought to shield us from the sun, and our day bags.

It was mid-day by the time we left the shop. Pablo took us to another shop where people were sitting at tables, eating.

'We'll have some lunch here,' he said. He then asked the shopkeeper to push enough tables together to allow us to sit down as a group. He told us the shop was called a cantina, and that it sold prepared food for eating on the premises.

The woman in charge of the shop gave us a list of dishes from which we could choose. Some things were familiar, but most we'd never heard of. Pablo said he would choose for all of us, and he explained what each item was as they arrived, in an apparently random order.

'This type of food is called 'Tapas',' he said. 'It's a traditional way of eating in the islands.'

Trevor William Poate

He selected a few things from some of the plates and transferred them to his own. We followed suit, and started eating. There were fishy things, bread, cheeses, spicy meats, pastes and…lots more. Some were hot, and some were cold. I didn't like everything, but did try them. We were all full, and feeling a little sleepy by the time the plates were empty.

'What's that man drinking?' I asked, pointing to someone at an adjacent table.

'It's called 'beer'. You can try it this evening,' he said, glancing at Robert and smiling in a strange manner. 'We have some back at the Centre.'

Our food shopping was different to the clothes shopping. Initially we bought some meat from shops, and then made our way to somewhere Pablo called the 'market'. As we entered, we bought some plastic tokens. They were given values of 1: 5, 10 and 20 credits. Pablo explained that the stallholders in the market didn't accept our identity cards for payment. Instead, we exchanged the tokens for the fruit and vegetables we wanted to buy. At the end of each day, the stallholders returned the tokens to the 'cashier' at the entrance where the credits were added to their monthly allowance.

Although in most places the food was grown on large controlled farms, it was common in small towns such as Orzola, for local people to farm small pieces of land and bring their produce to the market each day. Every type of vegetable or fruit had a fixed price according to the quantity bought. The only real choice was the quality.

Some items were sold by quantity, and some by weight. For example, chicken's eggs were sold individually, while rice was sold by weight. The market was bustling, with many people buying the fruit and vegetables, and carrying laden baskets.

The stalls were covered with thick material shading the produce from the sun, and built on a concrete floor. The sellers were mainly old women, most of whom looked poorer than any we'd seen elsewhere. Their clothes looked old and worn. They smiled at us as we walked past, encouraging us to buy their produce rather than anyone else's. They all seemed desperate to sell their produce before the end of the day.

'Why do these people look so poor?' Julia asked Pablo.

'When people stop working they receive a small credit allowance. They sometimes subsidise it by growing these fruits and vegetables, and selling them here. Markets like this are not regulated. We like to buy from here to help these people, but there are also regulated fruit and vegetable shops as well.'

'But I thought everyone was looked after.'

'Some are looked after more than others. The allowance is enough to live on, but if they want extras they need to earn more.'

It was the first time we'd heard of something not being regulated, apart from the Renegades.

The selection was much greater than we expected. Pablo explained about the items we didn't recognise, and arranged for us to taste a few of them. We also bought some dried spices in small plastic containers.

We bought as much as we thought we would need for the next few days, before finally heading to another shop where processed food was sold. We bought a few plastic containers of the pastes we'd had for lunch, some olive oil, and some pasta which was dried, unlike the pasta we'd made in the Quarantine Centre. Susan also recommended we buy a recipe book, which explained how to make some of the dishes we'd had for lunch.

We could barely carry everything as we slowly made our way back to the shuttle station. Our clothing was waiting for us on the platform, alongside the shuttle we would take back to the Centre. We loaded all our bags and sat, breathless, for a few minutes, before the shuttle departed at four o'clock.

Some of the Centre staff met us at our shuttle stop, and helped carry everything to our houses. We would have to cook for ourselves that evening, before meeting up in the main building. Pablo said he had some beer, and another drink called 'wine', for us to try that evening. He didn't explain what they were, he just smiled, in the same strange manner he had at lunch-time…

The feeling of mild euphoria from drinking alcohol for the first time was an enlightening experience. Wobbly legs and spinning rooms, combined with uncontrolled laughter made the evening one to remember! Calista and I certainly slept deeply afterwards, and woke later than usual the next morning, with a slight headache.

After breakfast we met the rest of the group in the main building, where Robert was waiting for us, with a broad grin on his face. Pablo was also there, but there was no sign of Mary or Susan.

'How are you this morning?' Robert asked, as we sat down.

'Better for having breakfast,' I said.

'Good. We have a busy day planned. This morning Pablo is going to teach you a few words of Spanish, just enough for your needs over the next few weeks. This afternoon we want you to go into Caleta del Sebo on your own, and buy a few things which we'll list out for you, and this evening we will all go back there for an evening's entertainment.'

'What sort of entertainment?' Abigail asked.

'You'll see this evening. Tomorrow is Sunday, so we will take you to a church to show you how a religious service is conducted, and on Monday we will take you to meet your work trainers in Arrecife. You will start three weeks work on the following Monday.'

'What will we do during the rest of next week?' Liam asked.

'Your work trainers will give you some lessons to do here, in preparation for your training. We will help you with them.'

Pablo told us to open a page on our workbooks, and we started the Spanish lesson. The words and phrases weren't particularly hard to learn, but the accent sounded strange, and there were more than a few laughs from him at our attempts to copy what he said. Some of the spellings seemed wrong to us. The letter 'J', was often pronounced as an 'H', which we found confusing, and some words ending in 'AY' were spelt with an 'E'. The most confusing letter was 'Z'. It was pronounced as 'TH', almost as though the person speaking was short tongued.

By lunchtime he was satisfied with our progress. He told us to practice in our houses for a couple of hours and meet him back there at two o'clock, when he would explain what he wanted us to buy in the town that afternoon. He asked Fabio and Tina to wait behind, saying he had some questions for them. I wondered what they were…

We caught the shuttle into the town, armed with our lists. We were supposed to buy a wicker shopping basket, some fish from the harbour, some freshly made bread and some cleaning items for our houses. We had never needed to clean anything before, and weren't too sure what we would do with the items after we'd bought them.

We were told to shop as couples, not as a group, and that Mary and Susan were already in the town, and would be watching us. Pablo told us the return train left the town at a quarter past four, which should give us long enough to buy everything.

Calista and I quickly found a shop selling the baskets, bought two, and then looked around the town for somewhere to buy the bread and cleaning items. We found a bread shop, which sold a variety of loaves and buns. We bought what we thought was enough for a week, not realising it would go hard after a day or so! That was our first mistake. Our second was buying a vast amount of cleaning soaps, liquids and powders. We had no idea how much we would need, and ended up buying enough for the whole group for the month we would be there! We were more successful in the harbour. There were many types of fish for sale, so we chose three different ones. The man selling them even took the bones out for us!

Convinced we had been successful in our task we returned to the Centre and displayed our goods to everyone. Only Fabio and Tina had bought just enough for their own needs, and were the stars of the afternoon. Strangely, they had known exactly what to buy and how much of each item.

'Are the fishermen regulated?' I asked Robert.

'Yes. The fishing boats bring their catch to a central warehouse where it is sorted, weighed, and distributed to the shops. Like the market, some retired people sell their own catches to subsidise their credit allowance.'

Pablo told us he would take the excess bread and cleaning items for the Centre's staff, so it wouldn't be wasted, then asked us to meet him at seven thirty for our evening's entertainment.

We cooked some of the fish and ate it with some

bread and butter for our evening meal, then showered, changed our clothes, and made our way to the main building. We were the last of the group to arrive. Susan, Mary, Pablo, and Robert were also there.

'We'll take the shuttle into the town and walk back later,' Robert said. 'The shuttle doesn't run after nine o'clock. It's not very far back here by foot, and will only take about half an hour.'

He went over to one of the tables where there was a plastic box, opened it, and took out a small tube with a glass front. 'Take one of these, each of you,' he said, switching one on and showing us the beam of light. 'It's called a 'torch', and will light the path back. It's basically a portable light, which uses rechargeable batteries to light the bulb.'

Each of us picked one up and pressed the button on the side, which switched it on. They were exactly the same, and much heavier than they looked.

'How long does the battery last?' Kevin asked.

'About four or five hours,' Robert replied, 'It only takes about an hour to recharge.'

We took the shuttle into the town, followed him along the main street and into a side road, and then entered a dimly lit room where local people were sitting, talking, and drinking wine and beer. Mary had booked a table for us, which we made our way to, and sat down on large cloth covered pillows, or cushions. There was a large empty area in the middle of the room, and a raised area at one end where two men and two women were sitting with a range of musical instruments. A man came up to us, put some tapas on the table, and asked what we would like to drink. Pablo and Robert ordered cervesa, (beer), and Mary and Susan ordered a bottle of vino, (wine). The rest of us looked at each other, remembering the previous evening, but not wanting to look out of place, we ordered the same.

We talked amongst ourselves for a while, before we noticed the room had gone quiet. The people on the platform started playing guitars, and one of the men began to sing. Pablo explained that the guitars were a type only found in Spain, that the music was traditional, and had been passed down from generation to generation. Very soon some of the local people stood up, moved towards the empty space in the middle of the room, and started moving in a peculiar manner.

'What are they doing?' Abigail asked Mary.

'Dancing,' she said.

We looked at each other in amazement. 'Come on, I'll show you how,' Pablo said to Abigail, taking her hand and pulling her to her feet.

They made their way onto the open floor and... started dancing. It wasn't very long before we were all doing it. The effects of the wine and beer had removed our inhibitions, and even though the local people must have thought us strange, they clapped and laughed as we gyrated along with them.

After about half an hour the music stopped, and everyone sat down, breathless. As we settled back onto our cushion, two couples dressed in odd looking clothes appeared from a side door. I recognised one of them as the man we'd bought our fish from that afternoon. The music started again and they began very slowly moving around the floor, speeding up as the music's tempo increased. They held some wooden disks in their hands, which they used to make a clacking noise, following the rhythm of the guitars.

'This is called flamenco dancing, and is traditional around here. The wooden disks in their hands are called castanets,' Pablo told us.

The dancing continued for about another quarter of an hour when the music stopped again. Everyone clapped their hands as it finished, and resumed their drinking and conversations. The dancing and floorshow was repeated twice more during the evening, and by eleven o'clock we were slightly intoxicated, tired, and ready to leave.

The crickets were rubbing their hind legs together and the night sky was clear, with no moon, just stars, as we started walking home, following Robert along a dark pathway using our torches to light it up. When we reached the Centre we went into the main building where Pablo, who'd gone on ahead of us, had opened some wine and had poured each of us a glassful.

We were all wobbly and slurring our words again by the time we went to bed. We could lie in the following morning because our church visit wasn't until the afternoon. Calista and I did sleep until late the next morning, very late.

Trevor William Poate

Robert had told us to wear some of our more formal, work style clothes for the church visit. He explained that it wasn't compulsory, but considered respectful. Having met him and the rest of the group in the main building, we walked into the town along the same path we had returned along the evening before.

As we neared the town, we could hear a bell ringing. Robert told us it was a Sunday tradition to ring the bell, as a call to prayer for the congregation. The church was a focal point of the town, being located in the main square. It was built of stone with few carvings, unlike the great cathedrals we'd seen pictures of. It had a tower where the bell was, and a clock showing the wrong time, suggesting it had stopped working a long time before. By the time we arrived it was busy, with people queuing up outside, and there was a man wearing a long white gown, shaking the hands of some of them as they entered. A large gold coloured cross hung by a chain around his neck.

We joined one of the queues and slowly moved forward towards the door. Inside it was dark, and there were tall white objects called 'candles', with a small flame at the top, flickering in the draft passing through the open doors. There were rows of benches, full to brimming with people, some sitting, some kneeling on cushions. We found a bench near the back, with enough space for us to sit together, and waited.

In a whisper, Robert explained about the various parts of the church, pointing out the altar, and a large cross with a man called Jesus hanging from it. Our religious lessons at the Quarantine Centre had explained the significance of most of the items, but we didn't know about the content of the mass. It was a Catholic church, which was part of what was called the Christian religion. The stone walls had very little decoration, but the windows, made from coloured glass depicting stories from the religious texts, were brightly lit by the sunshine outside.

The bell ringing came to a stop, and everyone stood up as an elderly man, dressed in a purple gown, appeared through a side door and made his way to the altar at the front. The Mass lasted for about an hour. We didn't understand very much of what was going on because it was conducted in Spanish, but whenever the priest spoke, the congregation listened in silence, hanging on to his every word. Near the end of the Mass, the whole congregation, apart from us, queued up to receive a wafer and a sip of red wine, representing the bread of life and the blood of Jesus. The Christian religions believed that Jesus was the son of their God, who spent time on earth in the 'Holy Land', what is now called Israel, preaching the word of God, his 'Father'. The last Middle East War came to mind.

We were amongst the first to leave after the mass had finished. Robert said we should go straight back to the Centre, and he led the way along the path. During the walk, he asked us for our thoughts on the Mass. It was difficult to say. Clearly, the congregation took their religion very seriously, but none of us could really empathise with it.

'Aren't The Middle Eastern religions mainly Muslim and Jewish?' I said.

'Yes, they are,' he replied.

'Then why do the Christians worship someone who lived there?'

'The Christian religion is derived from the Jewish religion. The main difference is, that the Jews don't believe that Jesus was the 'Son of God'. They believe he was simply a prophet. When he was alive he was worshipped by some people as 'Christ, King of the Jews', which caused him to be persecuted, and eventually crucified by the authorities, because they thought he was a threat to them. You should read up on it if you are interested, but you were told a lot of this in the Quarantine Centre.'

'What does crucified mean?'

'He was nailed to a wooden cross and left to die. That's why the Cross, or Crucifix, is worn by most Christians around their necks. You saw a large one above the altar in the church.'

'I still don't understand.'

'The Christians believe he died to save them.'

I thought about what he'd said, but still didn't really understand why someone would die to save other people, or how their death could save them.

'I wonder what is happening in the Complex,' Calista said, as we ate our meal that evening on the roof of our house.

'The same as always, I suppose,' I replied.

'Don't you think it's unfair that they know nothing of life outside?'

I paused, thinking. 'But, as they reach middle age they will all leave when they stop parenting, and live like us.'

'Yes. I suppose they will, but they'll never see their families or grandchildren.'

'No, they won't.'

We finished our food, and cleared away the dishes, ready to go to bed.

'Have you noticed anything strange here?' Calista said. I could tell from her voice that something was bothering her.

'Such as?' I said.

'There are no children, only a few babies…'

Chapter 3

Work Training

*W*e met the rest of the group in the main building at nine o'clock, wearing our new work clothes. I felt stiff, and uncomfortable. Robert, Pablo and Susan were waiting for us.

'Julia,' Robert said, 'you will go with Susan to the Nursing Centre this morning. Fabio, Abigail and Callum, you will go with Pablo to the Technical Centre, and the rest of you will come with me to the Education Centre. The visits will last most of the day. During the rest of the week we will prepare you for your three weeks work-training in your respective jobs.'

'Where will we be working?' Julia asked.

'In Arrecife, the capital of Lanzarote.'

'How far away is that?'

'About thirty kilometres from Orzola. We'll take the shuttle to Orzola, and then catch another one to Arrecife. It's about half an hour's journey from Orzola.'

'Are the Centres in the same place?' I asked.

'No. They are all in Arrecife, but in different parts of the city.'

'So I won't be working with Calista.'

'No, you won't.'

Calista and I looked at each other. We'd always worked together in the Complex, so working separately was going to be strange.

'We should get going,' Pablo said, 'The shuttle will arrive soon.'

We took the shuttle to Orzola, and boarded another one to Arrecife. It passed through a town called Haria, and then another called Teguise and arrived in Arrecife at ten thirty.

We split up into our groups and walked to our respective Centres. The Technical Centre was a large four level building, a short walk from the station. It appeared to be quite new, and had an array of satellite dishes on the roof. Pablo took us to a reception area, where our ID cards were checked and we were given a temporary access badge. We took a lift to the fourth level, where we were met by a young woman who introduced herself as Sylvia. She told us she was in charge of training, and we would be working with her when we started the following week. I guessed she knew who we were and where we'd come from, because she referred to the systems we'd used in the Complex as being very similar to the ones we would learn about, but of a much older design. She didn't actually mention the Complex by name, just referred to it as 'where we'd been before'.

We spent the morning looking around the building, and meeting a few of the technicians we would be working with. After a quick lunch, we went to a training room where she explained how the training would be conducted. She told us the page numbers and access codes on our workbooks for the preparatory work we would be doing at the Rehabilitation Centre during the rest of the week. She also told us she expected us to be competent in the basics by the time we started our work training the following Monday.

By four o'clock we were back at the shuttle station, and we met up with the others for our journey back to Graciosa.

'How did you get on?' I asked Calista, as the shuttle started moving.

'I now know where all the children are,' she replied.

'What do you mean?'

'From the age of two, they live in the Education Centre. They're only allowed to visit their parents three times a year.'

'What's it like?'

'The buildings are pleasant enough, the children all have a nice place to live, and the facilities are really good. I've a lot to learn but, well, I thought it a little, how can I say…confined. They seem happy, and have everything they need, but it wasn't what I expected. Parents see more of their children in the Complex than they do here.'

'I've also a lot of things to learn. The systems are similar to those we had in the Complex, but newer. But…I don't know, I thought it would be more interesting. What they do seems very routine. I know it was like that in the Complex, but we didn't have any choice there. We were trying to survive.'

Julia briefly told us about the Nursing Centre. It too had more modern equipment than in the Complex. She told us that the medical procedures were more advanced than she'd been used to, although her nursing duties were similar, and there were new drugs she'd never heard of.

Only Calista and I seemed subdued by what we'd seen.

By the time we arrived back at the Centre we were ready to eat. Robert told us to meet him the next morning in the main building at eight o'clock, when we would start our lessons. We went back to our houses to prepare our food. Neither Calista nor I were particularly happy about our prospective futures. We talked late into the evening about what we'd seen, and what we might expect when we were finally relocated. We also talked about the Renegades: where they might be, and how they might live.

The moon had reappeared as a small crescent in the night sky.

We spent most of the rest of the week on the lessons we'd been given. By Friday afternoon, Robert was satisfied with our progress and suggested we spend the evening in the town, at the cantina. The evening followed the same pattern as our previous visit, although Calista and I didn't join the others for wine when we returned to the Centre, preferring to have an early night. Robert told us we should go to Orzola the following morning to do some food shopping, and that the rest of the weekend was free to do anything we wanted. He made a few suggestions, such as exploring the parts of Graciosa we hadn't seen, and going for a swim in the sea on the Sunday afternoon. We couldn't swim, and the idea of submerging ourselves in the sea water was a little disconcerting. Susan and Pablo said they would go with us, just to make sure we didn't get into any trouble in the water. Fabio and Tina said they didn't want to go, but the rest of us agreed we would. I asked Susan what we should wear for swimming, and she replied that we didn't need to wear anything, as long as we used one of the more secluded beaches they would show us. I'd obviously seen Calista naked, but the idea of us cavorting on a beach, and in the sea without any clothes, was a big surprise. When it came to it, it seemed the most natural thing to do! Nobody was embarrassed. The seawater was warm and invigorating, and our skins were beginning to darken where exposed to the sun. Susan gave us some cream to apply to our white areas to stop us burning. Most of our skin was white!

By the Sunday evening we were relaxed and ready for our first day's work in Arrecife.

Pablo, Susan and Robert accompanied us on the first day. Because we were staying so far from our work places, we weren't expected to start and finish at the same time as the other workers. They started at eight thirty and finished at five thirty. We arrived at nine thirty and were allowed to leave at four thirty.

We split into our groups at the station and walked the short distance to our respective work centres. Sylvia was waiting for us in the entrance as we arrived at the Technical Centre. She took us to the training room where there were two men and two women waiting for us. She introduced us, and allocated one of them to each of us, explaining we would be working with that particular person during our time there. My trainer was a woman called Diana. She was in her mid forties, very pleasant, and appeared helpful. After a few words of welcome from Sylvia, we left and made our way to our workstations.

During the following two weeks I got to know Diana quite well. She had been born on Lanzarote, and brought up in the Education Centre where Calista was working. She had two children with her partner, who ran a food shop in Arrecife. I quizzed her about her children, particularly their confinement at the Education Centre. She seemed confused that I thought it strange they didn't live with her. I didn't know how much she knew about our past, so didn't pursue the subject. She gave me the impression she thought we had been temporarily transferred from another region, for a short period of training. She had clearly never met anyone from the Complex before, and I wondered who had retrained previous people.

She was a very attentive teacher, and I learned about the systems very quickly. By the end of the second week I was working on my own, only occasionally needing her assistance. I didn't enjoy the routine work, and hoped it would be more interesting when I got to my new work, wherever that might be.

Calista was becoming increasingly depressed. She didn't like seeing the children confined, and was struggling with dealing with them person to person, particularly when she had to tell them to behave. In the Complex, she had taught using the holographic link, and never actually met them face to face. She wanted to be their friend, not their master.

Susan was becoming concerned about Calista, and asked her what was wrong. Calista told her she thought the children should be allowed to live with their parents, and go to the Education Centre every day, rather than live there, confined. She was sympathetic to Calista's views, but explained that the system had been developed over many years and had been proven to be the best for the children's education and welfare.

Calista and I were not convinced. We spent hours discussing what we'd learnt and seen, and our general situation, without arriving at any conclusions. I'd never seen her so unhappy, confused and…unsettled.

'I want to know more about the Renegades,' she said, on the Sunday after our second week at work. We were sitting on our roof, eating dinner. 'Do you think they live like we do?'

'I don't know. I suppose we can ask, but I don't think we'll be told.'

'We need to find out where they live. Perhaps we

could ask at work.' She spoke with an urgency I'd never heard before.

'Even if we do find out, we won't be allowed to go there.'

'But if we find out where they are, we might be able to go there ourselves.'

'How?'

'I don't know. I wish I did,' she said, her voice faltering.

'If you really want to leave, we'll find a way.'

She came over to me, put her arms around my waist and, looking into my eyes, said. 'Will we?'

'Yes, we will, somehow.'

The following day I decided to ask Diana what she knew about the Renegades. I didn't expect her to know very much, or tell me anything, but it was worth a try.

'Diana, have you ever met any Renegades?' I asked during lunch.

'Renegades, why?'

'I'm just curious.'

'I've never met any, but I do know that some live on one of the islands.'

'Which islands?'

'These islands.'

'How many islands are there here?'

'Seven inhabited ones, and a few more uninhabited ones.'

'Which one has the Renegades?'

'It's called El Hierro. It's south west of here.'

'I didn't think they lived anywhere near other people.'

'Why not?'

'I thought they were outcasts.'

'Well, they are, and they're not. They were given El Hierro to keep them away from the rest of us, but they do occasionally visit some of the other islands.'

'What for?'

'They do a little bartering, and occasionally, if one of them is very ill, they get treatment at one of the hospitals. They're not supposed to, but the doctors turn a blind eye. After all, they are people too.'

'What do you mean by 'barter'. I've never heard that word before.'

'It just means swapping, or exchanging, things. For example, if they need medicines, they might exchange some food products for them. We're not supposed to barter with them, but some people do.'

'Are any of them deformed?'

'Deformed? Why do you ask that?'

'Someone told me they have deformities.'

'I don't think so, but some may have.'

'So, how do they survive?'

'The island has a wind farm providing electricity, and reservoirs for fresh water. They grow their own crops, keep some cows and goats, and they fish. They build their own houses and, I'm told, they have a Community Government, a school, and a basic Medical Centre using natural remedies.

'How many people live on the island?'

'I'm not sure. I think it's around six thousand.'

'Six thousand!'

'Yes, I think so.'

'Do people from the other islands ever visit them?'

'No. It's not allowed.'

'But if someone wanted to go there, could they?'

'I suppose so, but they would need to find someone with a boat to take them. It's against the law, and very risky.'

'Which island would they go from?'

'Tenerife. Why are you asking about them?'

'Calista was curious.'

'If I were you, I'd tell her not to be. If any government officials find out you are asking questions about them, you'll get into trouble.'

'Why?'

'You just will, believe me. We'd better get back to work now.'

'One more thing. How far is the island from here?'

'I don't know. I've never been there. Now, back to work,' she said, standing up.

'Yes. Alright.'

I waited until we were back in our house that evening, before telling Calista what I'd learnt.

'I asked Alfred as well,' she said. Alfred was her trainer at the Education Centre.

'What did he say?'

'He said I shouldn't be asking about them.'

'So did Diana.'

'Do you think we could escape, and go there?'

'We don't know how far it is, or who would take us.'

'But if we could get to Tenerife, we might be able to find someone to take us. Or maybe one of the Renegades might be visiting, and agree to take us.' She was beginning to get excited at the idea, and so was I.

'But how would we get to Tenerife?' I said.

'I don't know. We need to ask a few more people.'

'Ask who?'

'Perhaps we could ask some of the fishermen in the harbour here? They know about boats.'

I paused for a few moments, thinking. 'We don't have very long. We're supposed to leave here in ten days.'

'I know.'

'There are ferry boats in Arrecife. Perhaps we could ask there if any go to Tenerife.'

'When?'

'Saturday would be the best day. We can tell Robert we are going to Arrecife to do some shopping.'

'Do you think he'll believe us?'

'We can try, but if we get caught, we could be in serious trouble with him.'

'What can he do to us?' she said, glancing towards the main building.

'I don't know.'

Trevor William Poate

'Do you think we are being watched?'

'I don't think so, but there's something about Fabio and Tina that's been worrying me. They both seem overly interested whenever we mention the Renegades. I wonder if they've been telling Robert what we are talking about. Also, they seem to talk privately with him a lot.'

We sat silently for a few minutes, thinking about all the problems.

'One more thing. What if we don't like it there?' I said.

'I don't like it here, and we'll be free…'

We spent the rest of the evenings that week talking about what we would do on the Saturday. I had managed to get a map of Arrecife showing us where the harbour for the ferries was located. I also asked Sylvia about the Renegades, but she wasn't much more help than Diana had been, and also warned me not to ask too many questions.

Friday was our last day at work. Robert, Pablo and Susan accompanied us and we spent time with our trainers, discussing our progress. Apart from a few minor things, we had learnt everything we would need in our new work. That evening, Robert told us that we would receive our final training when we reached our new living location.

I knew that Calista and I needed Robert's agreement to go to Arrecife the following day, because we would need to use some of our credits for the shuttle journey, and our credit spending was monitored. He seemed surprised when I asked him.

'Why do you want to spend the day in Arrecife?' he asked.

'We haven't had any time to look around,' I said, avoiding his stare.

He spoke quietly with Mary for a few moments, and then said. 'We could all go as a group. Does anyone else want to spend the day there?' He looked around the room.

'We'll go,' Kevin said, looking at Julia.

'And the rest of you?' Mary said, glancing around the room.

Liam and Fabio nodded, after glancing at Abigail and Tina. 'Yes, alright we'll go as well,' Fabio said.

It was not what Calista and I wanted. We knew it would be difficult to ask about the boats to Tenerife if we were being chaperoned.

'Can we look around by ourselves?' I asked.

Robert looked unsure. 'Why do you want to do that?'

'So we can get used to meeting people and being independent,' I said, rather unconvincingly.

'We'll decide tomorrow.'

There was nothing more to say. Somehow we would have to get some time on our own. Our plans were now in tatters.

'One last thing,' Robert said, as we were getting up to go back to our houses, 'You will be leaving here on

Wednesday. On Monday I'll brief each of you on where you are going. You'll need to pack all your belongings by Tuesday evening because you'll be leaving early.'

'Can't you tell us now?' Julia asked.

'I won't know myself until Monday, so no, I can't.'

Chapter 4

The Arrangements

*W*e arrived in Arrecife early the next day. Only Robert and Mary accompanied the eight of us. They must have discussed the visit the previous evening, because they told us they would show us around the town and then, in the afternoon, we could spend two hours on our own, and meet them back at the cantina where we would be having lunch. I was worried that two hours wouldn't be long enough to find out about the ferries, but it was all the time we had.

The morning seemed to last forever. They showed us around a museum of ancient artefacts in an old castle, a park, and some shops where we bought a few clothes. We had lunch in a cantina near the sea front, not too far from the harbour. By two o'clock, we were on our own, at last.

Calista and I casually left the cantina, and as soon as we thought we were out of sight, almost ran the short distance to the harbour. There were hundreds of boats, and we didn't know where to start. We wandered around until Calista saw a sign advertising tickets. We joined a short queue and, when it came to our turn, asked about ferries to Tenerife. To our surprise, the man behind the counter simply gave us a piece of paper listing all the ferry routes, the sailing times and the prices. It was exactly what we wanted. The ferry to Tenerife left at eleven o'clock every day, arriving twelve hours later. The problem was the price. It was one thousand credits. We didn't know how many credits we had left from our original five thousand, and were unsure how to find out.

It had taken far less time than we expected to find out about the ferry, so we wandered around for a while, bought a few items of food to make it look as though we had simply been shopping, and returned to the cantina where Robert and Mary were waiting.

'You've been quick,' Mary said, in a sarcastic voice, as we sat down at their table.

'We saw most things we wanted to this morning,' I said, glancing at Calista. 'Also, we don't know how many credits we have left, so didn't know what we could buy.'

'The last time I checked, a few days ago, you had about five hundred credits each,' Robert said.

'Is that all?' Calista replied.

'At the moment.'

'When will we get some more?' I asked.

'I am going to credit you with another five thousand on Monday. That should give you enough for what you need,' he said, glancing at Mary in a peculiar way.

I looked at Calista. If we were going to escape, it would have to be on the Tuesday. We had hoped to go on the Monday, but couldn't be sure the credits would be there.

'Do we only have packing to do on Tuesday?' I asked.

'Yes. You can go to the beach if you have time, but otherwise we have nothing planned for you.'

'How will we leave the island?' Calista asked.

'It depends on where you are going. We'll know your route on Monday. Some of you may go back to El Quatia by boat, and some of you may fly out of here,' Mary said, looking at Robert suspiciously.

'Fly?'

'Yes. If you are going to Europe, you'll have to fly. The boat journey is too long, and you may be living inland somewhere.'

We knew aircraft existed and that they were only used for government business, but had never seen one.

'I didn't know aircraft came here.' I said.

'They do, but not very often.'

'Where do they land?'

'The airport isn't far from here.'

'Have you ever flown?'

'I have,' Robert said, looking directly at me.

'So have I, twice,' Mary said.

'What's it like?' Calista asked.

'Imagine if you are a bird, floating in the sky, looking down on the land. Everything is tiny, and looks like children's toys.'

Liam and Abigail arrived and sat down next to us. The conversation turned to what they had been doing, and by the time the others had also arrived, we were ready to leave. Fabio and Tina held back and spoke quietly to Mary. I wondered what they were saying.

Because it was our last Saturday at the Centre, we all agreed to go to the cantina for the evening. We ate tapas again, danced, and drank too much alcohol. It didn't matter though; we had nothing planned for the Sunday.

We were at the beach on our own during the Sunday afternoon. 'I've been thinking,' I said to Calista, 'if we do go on Tuesday, we won't be able to take very much with us.'

'I know,' she said, 'but apart from a few clothes, and things we brought from the Complex, we don't have very much anyway.'

'We can't take our bags; we'll have to use the baskets.'

'Why can't we use the bags?'

'Someone might see us leaving with them, and ask why. If we just put a few things in the baskets, we can say we are coming here.'

'What time will we have to leave?'

'Early. The eight o'clock shuttle.'

'Won't they think it's a bit early to be coming to the beach?'

I thought for a few moments, and said. 'We could pack the baskets tomorrow, hide them on the path to the shuttle station, and collect them when we go. That way we won't be seen carrying anything. We could just say we are going for a walk.'

'We could hide our bags instead. No one is going to check the house to see if we still have them.'

'If we get up very early on Tuesday we could walk to the station before anyone else is awake, and catch the six thirty shuttle. That would give us plenty of time.'

'Do you think so?' she said, holding my hand in a tight grip.

'Let me think about it some more.'

Robert had told us to meet him in the main building after lunch on Monday, when he would tell us the arrangements for our departure. He was waiting for us with Mary when we arrived. I wondered where Pablo and Susan were.

'Good afternoon everyone. I've received the notification of your relocation and travel arrangements,' he said. He paused, waiting for some reaction from us. None of us spoke. There was an anticipatory atmosphere between us.

'Kevin and Julia. You will be going by air to your placement in England. Liam and Abigail. You will be going to Ireland on the same flight as Kevin and Julia. Fabio and Tina; you will be going to Italy by boat and shuttle. The details are on your workbooks and the page numbers and codes are on these sheets of paper,' he said, passing out a sheet to each couple. 'Finally, Callum and Calista. You are staying here for a while. Are there any questions?'

'Yes,' I said. 'Why are we staying here?'

'I'll explain afterwards. The rest of you can go and read your instructions, and start getting your belongings together. You'll be leaving early on Wednesday morning.'

Calista and I waited while the others left. They were talking animatedly to each other, excited, as they headed out of the building, glancing in our direction as they passed us. I wondered if any of them knew why we weren't leaving.

'Alright. Callum; Calista. As part of your rehabilitation we've been monitoring your progress,' Robert said, after the others had left us. He sounded... unhappy...dejected. 'Unfortunately there have been a few things we're not happy about. We've been listening to some of your conversations in your house, and we know you've been asking about the Renegades.'

'How do you know what we've been talking about?' I asked.

'We have microphones in all the houses. We listen to everyone. Also, Diana, Sylvia and Alfred mentioned your conversations in their reports about you.'

I looked at Calista. She appeared as stunned as I was.

'Who else has been telling you things?' Calista said.

'Who else do you think?'

'Fabio and Tina?'

Mary was quiet for a moment, before saying. 'I think you're being a little paranoid.'

'What are you going to do with us?' I asked.

'We've recommended to the Federal Government that you are sent to a Detention Centre, where you will be kept until they think you can be trusted to be released into the community. We are just waiting for confirmation of our recommendation, and your travel arrangements.'

'What is a Detention Centre?' Calista asked.

'It's a closed community where you will be…'persuaded'… to conform to the rules for living in an open community,' Mary said, in a voice devoid of any emotion.

'Persuaded? What does that mean?'

'It means you'll be subject to further training, and psychological evaluation, designed to dissuade you from trying to join the Renegades, and to conform to life in an open community.'

'What if we're not persuaded?' I asked.

'You'll stay there until you are.'

'What will happen if we're not?'

'You will be, sooner or later.'

'Where is this place?'

'That's of no importance at the moment.'

Robert looked at Mary, and said. 'This is the first time we've made this recommendation. It wasn't easy for us. I'm sorry, but we cannot allow you to join the Renegades, or disrupt your new community.'

'All we want to do is have children and live a free life. Everything is controlled here. We're just like dolls or puppets, dancing to your tune. We can't make any

Trevor William Poate

decisions of any importance. You tell us where to live, where to work and how to behave. That can't be natural,' Calista said, in an emotional voice.

'You don't understand how things work on the outside.'

'Tell us.'

'I'm sorry, but that's how the world works. We can't explain any more than we already have. We've tried very hard to help you but…you don't seem to want to conform,' Robert said. He appeared to understand our arguments, but we could tell by Mary's face that she was not at all sympathetic towards us.

'It doesn't work like that for the Renegades,' Calista said. She was clearly upset at the news, and Mary's attitude.

'They are not free either, and they also have rules and regulations. They can't go where they like and they don't have the benefits available to everyone else,' Mary said, in a voice which suggested she thought we were just a nuisance.

'What benefits?'

'All the benefits the Federal Government provides for us. Housing: work, medical care, plenty of food and clothing, and security.'

'Security?' Calista said, her voice rising. 'You mean control. That's your idea of security. We are denied any freedom of choice. We have no rights.'

Robert looked at Mary and said. 'Calista, please calm down. The world is…it is as it is.'

'You are fools. You all just do what you're told,' Calista shouted.

'That's enough,' Mary shouted back, as Calista started crying. 'That's all we can tell you for now. We'll tell you when we know your arrangements, probably tomorrow. Go to your house, the town or the beach, but don't try and leave the island.'

We took that as a threat. Mary was clearly angry by Calista's outburst. There was nothing else we could say. We left them and started walking back to our house, my arm around Calista's shoulders. She was still sobbing.

'I think we should go to the beach, they can't overhear us there,' I said, gesturing to her to be quiet, by putting a finger up to my lips.

'We don't know that,' she said, equally quietly, tears running down her cheeks.

I took her hand, and said. 'It's less likely than in the house.'

'Alright.'

We briefly called into the house to collect our towels, and made our way to the beach. We deliberately sat away from the edge of the beach where there were bushes and rocks, because we thought it safer to talk without being overheard. After a quick swim in the water, we returned to our towels and sat down.

'What do we do now?' Calista said, as I dried myself. 'They seem to know everything we do.'

'Did you notice, they didn't mention that we'd been to the ticket office for the ferries? Perhaps they don't know.'

'It doesn't matter. They'll be watching us to make sure we don't try to leave.'

'They can't watch us all the time,' I said, looking along the beach where the waves were lapping the shoreline. 'I wonder how many of them will take the rest of the group to the airport and the ferry on Wednesday.'

'Why?'

'If they all go, we'll be here on our own.'

'I doubt if they'll all go,' she said, following my gaze along the beach.

'You're probably right, but if they do, it will give us a chance to escape.'

'What if we have to leave on Wednesday?'

'I think we'll be here for a few more days.'

'If they do all go, it'll give us our only chance.'

'We'd have to leave everything behind. We couldn't risk taking any bags.'

We sat silently for a while, thinking about our chances of escape. They didn't seem very good. About twenty minutes later, we saw Kevin and Julia walking towards us. They came and sat down next to us, and asked us why we weren't leaving with them. I explained what Robert and Mary had told us, about them monitoring our conversations, and us being sent to a Detention Centre because we'd asked about the Renegades.

'Have they been listening to all of us?' Julia asked.

'I think so,' I said.

She sounded worried as she said. 'We've said

some things that we wouldn't have said if we'd known we were being overheard.'

'What things?'

'Well, we've talked about how little real freedom we have. We expected more once we left the Complex, but life still seems controlled,' she replied, looking at Kevin.

'Yes. We thought we would be allowed to live how we wanted, within some rules of course, but that doesn't seem to be the case,' he said.

'You have never told us why you were expelled from the Complex,' Calista said.

Kevin looked at Julia, and said. 'We were told not tell anyone. But I don't suppose it matters now. Julia found out about the twins, and threatened to tell other people we met on our Community Day. She worked for a while in the Maternity Centre, and saw what was happening. She questioned one of the doctors about it and, within a day, we were sent to the Quarantine Centre. They told us we were a risk.'

'Why do they think you are not a risk now?' I asked.

'I suppose it doesn't matter out here. No one in the Complex knew about the twins, at least, no one apart from the Officers and medical staff.'

'Where do the twins go?' Calista asked.

'They are sent to the Eugenics Centre. ' Julia said.

'What's that?'

'It's a wing attached to the Medical Centre. I've never been there.'

Trevor William Poate

'Patricia told us they are fostered outside.'

'I think there's more to it than that.'

'What do you mean?'

'I think they are used for experiments.'

Calista and I were shocked at the idea. 'What sort of experiments?' I said.

'Medical experiments.'

'Such as?'

'Trying out new drugs, and medical procedures.'

'So they are used as guinea pigs,' Calista said.

'Yes, sort of.'

'What are you going to do now?' Kevin asked.

Calista looked at me, before saying. 'We're thinking of trying to escape and joining the Renegades. There's an island not too far from here where there's about six thousand of them.'

'How can you escape?'

'There are ferries from Arrecife to an island called Tenerife. The other island, where some of the Renegades live, isn't far from there.'

'When are you going?' Julia said, looking at me.

'We had planned to go tomorrow, but I don't think we can now. We've been told not to try to leave the island, so I'm sure we are being watched,' I said.

'Do you think so?' Kevin said, looking around.

'Yes, we do,' Calista said, following Kevin's gaze.

'What time do you leave on Wednesday?' I asked him.

'Early. We are catching the first shuttle, at six

thirty, with Liam and Abigail. I don't know when Tina and Fabio are leaving.'

'Who is going with you?'

'I don't know. Probably Robert. Why?'

'I just wondered.'

We talked for a while before going for another swim. It was very hot, and the cool water was refreshing. Kevin and Julia joined us, and by late afternoon, we left the beach and walked back to our houses. There was a note on the door, telling us we would all be eating together that evening in the main building. Neither Calista nor I wanted to go, but Mary called in to see us, and made it clear we didn't have a choice. It seemed they were keeping a closer watch on us than we thought.

The next morning we again made our way to the beach, as we had nothing else to do. Susan was already there when we arrived. We hadn't seen her the previous evening, and were surprised she wasn't working somewhere.

'What are you doing here?' I asked, as we sat down next to her.

'I have a rest day,' she replied.

'You're not here to keep an eye on us, are you?'

'No. I'm not. I heard about you being sent to a Detention Centre. I'm sorry. I've never known it happen before.'

Calista and I undressed, and lay down on our towels next to her.

Trevor William Poate

'Robert tells me you want to join the Renegades,' she said.

I looked at Calista, and said. 'It's got to be better than the Detention Centre.'

She was quiet for a few moments, and then said. 'I could help you, if you want.'

'Help us. How?'

'Robert, Mary, and Pablo will go with the others tomorrow morning. I've been told to stay here and watch you, but I can't watch you all the time, can I?'

'What are you saying?' Calista asked.

'Just that, if you were to catch the eight o'clock shuttle, I might think you're still in your house. I might not know you've left.'

I looked at Calista. Her face had a shocked look on it. 'Why would you do that?' I said.

'I don't think you deserve to be sent to a Detention Centre, and neither does Pablo. It's Mary who wants you sent there. We argued against it, but she is adamant.'

'Won't you get into trouble?' I said.

'Yes we will, but we'd rather that than see you in a Detention Centre. We are leaving here in a week, and are being replaced by Ronaldo and Patricia. You know them from the Quarantine Centre. By then we'll be long gone.'

'Gone where?'

'We have a weeks break before going to the Quarantine Centre to work for a few months.'

She paused for a few moments, appearing to think about what to say next. 'Pablo's going to Arrecife this afternoon. He'll bring you two ferry tickets this evening, for tomorrow's ferry to Tenerife. If you buy them, Mary and Robert will know where you've gone, from your credit records. That's why he's buying them for you.'

'What about when we get to Tenerife? How will we get to El Hierro'?'

'You'll have to do that yourself. All I can tell you is, you will need to make your way to Los Gigantes in the southwest of the island. I'm told that's where the Renegades go when they visit.'

'Won't we be caught if we use our credits?'

'Pablo will give you new ID cards. They will have your names and photo's, but different identity codes. They should be good for about a week. Once the Regional Government finds out about them, they'll be cancelled.'

'Will that be enough time?'

'It's all the time you'll have.'

She stood up and said. 'I'm going for a swim. Tell me what you want to do when I come back, then I'll tell Pablo. He'll be going after lunch, so make up your minds before then. Just remember, you can't do it without our help.'

She strolled down to the edge of the water, and started wading in. We watched her naked, tanned body, in silence.

'Do you think it's a trick?' Calista said.

'I don't know, but it's a chance we have to take.'

She swam for about half an hour, returned to us, and sat down on her towel.

'Have you made up your minds?' she said.

'Yes. We'll do it,' I said.

'Alright, I'll tell Pablo.' Her skin was already dry from the hot sun. 'I'll go now, and be back in about an hour. Don't leave here and don't talk to Fabio and Tina. They are Senior Security Officers, and have been reporting on you to Mary and Robert.'

'No, we won't,' I said, looking at Calista. 'I thought there was something strange about them, but Mary said they hadn't been telling her anything.'

'They will be returning to the Quarantine Centre tomorrow, not going to Italy. The Officers use them to monitor people during their retraining.'

She stood up, put some loose clothes on, and made her way back along the beach towards the Centre. Calista and I went for a swim, while we waited.

Pablo brought us the tickets and new identity cards that evening. We thanked him, but he didn't reply. He just smiled, and left us.

Chapter 5

Freedom

Calista and I were nervous the next morning as we looked out of our living room window, waiting for the rest of the group to leave. Soon after six o'clock, we saw them, carrying their belongings. We had said our farewells the previous evening, not letting on that we knew about Fabio and Tina, and were careful not to be seen watching them go. For Susan's plan to work, we needed to appear to be still asleep, so she could say she hadn't seen us that morning.

We had decided to take one small bag of belongings each, and had packed them the previous evening. We had over an hour to wait before we made our escape. Neither of us felt hungry, but we knew we should eat some breakfast because we didn't know if we could get food on the ferry.

We walked to the shuttle station soon after half past seven. There was no one around, and I wondered if Susan had deliberately told the Centre's staff to stay indoors. The shuttle was nearly full when it arrived. We sat on the side facing away from the harbour, because we needed to be careful not to be seen when the shuttle stopped there. Robert would be there with Fabio and Tina, and they might be watching. We safely passed through the harbour and were soon crossing the causeway to Orzola, our hearts thumping with excitement, and the fear of being caught.

There was a thirty minute wait in Orzola for the shuttle to Arrecife. We bought our tickets using our new identity cards, hoping nothing would go wrong, and stood in a corner of the station trying to be invisible, while we waited for it to arrive. We didn't know anyone there and had no reason to worry, but we did anyway.

I noticed a long-haired man wandering around the station, occasionally glancing in our direction. He was wearing fishermen's clothes and carrying a small bag. I pointed him out to Calista. We hadn't seen him before, but he seemed to be interested in us. When the shuttle arrived we got on, and so did he.

By the time we reached Arrecife, at about half past nine, we were feeling more confident. We walked from the shuttle station to the harbour, asked someone where we would find the ferry, and were aboard half an hour before it was due to leave. We found our seats, and settled down for the long journey, breathing a sigh of relief at how easy it had been.

Just before the boat was ready to leave, the long-haired man boarded and took a seat a few rows ahead of us.

'It's that man again,' I said to Calista.

She looked at where I was pointing, and said. 'Do

you think he's following us?'

'Why should he?'

'Perhaps he works for Mary, and she knows we are trying to escape,' she replied, in a whisper.

At precisely eleven o'clock, we felt the boat start to move. It slowly left the harbour and headed out to sea, speeding up as soon as it reached open water. The boat was much bigger than the one we'd arrived on from El Quatia. There were some open deck areas, which we had a look around, and shops where people were buying food, but for most of the journey we stayed in our seats, trying to look as inconspicuous as possible, but keeping an eye on the long-haired man.

We were both very tired when the boat started slowing down to negotiate the entrance to the port of Santa Cruz on Tenerife. We looked out of the windows, but all we could see were shadows of buildings with yellow dots of light. We would have to find somewhere to stay and, if possible, something to eat.

As soon as the boat was tied up at the dock, people started queuing to get off. We joined the back of the queue and slowly made our way down the metal gangway. We didn't have any idea where to go, so followed some of the other passengers along a street which eventually led to what appeared to be a shopping area. There were people still sitting outside cantinas, despite the late hour, drinking beer and wine. We stopped at one cantina and asked a waiter if there was anywhere we could stay. The long-haired man was sitting at the bar.

'It's that man again,' Calista said.

I looked at the bar, where he was sitting. He glanced at me, then turned back to his drink.

The waiter pointed along the road and said there were a few small hotels we could choose from and suggested the name of one in particular. We followed his directions and found the hotel he'd named. It looked alright from the outside. We went inside where an old woman was sitting behind a table, and asked her if we could stay for the night. She said she had a room and told us the price. It was just past midnight when we paid and asked her if we could get any food. She said there was none there, but some of the cantinas were still serving. Although we were hungry, we didn't want to go back out, so went to bed and slept for the first time as free people.

Calista woke me early the next morning. The sun was shining through the small window overlooking the street. I glanced outside where there were people sitting at tables outside a cantina, having their breakfast. The long-haired man was sitting at one of them, eating. I pointed him out to Calista.

'He's everywhere we go,' she said.

I didn't reply. I was worried, but didn't want to alarm her. We washed and dressed, and made our way down the stairs to the dining room where food was laid out on a table. The old woman we'd seen the night before told us to help ourselves to breakfast and that it was included in the price of the room. We ate enough for four people.

I asked the woman where the shuttle station was, because we wanted to go to Los Gigantes. She gave us a strange look and asked why we wanted to go there. I told her we had been told it was an interesting place to go.

She laughed, and said. 'If you like strange people.'

'What do you mean?' I said.

'You'll see when you get there. Why are you here? You are not with the Federal Government, are you?'

I looked at Calista, and said. 'No, we are just travelling, looking for some freedom.'

'Freedom! There is no freedom.' She paused, her eyes glazing over, as though she was remembering when she had been free. 'How long do you have?'

'A week. We came from Lanzarote, yesterday.'

'Lanzarote? You came on the ferry.'

'Yes we did.'

Her strange look reappeared. 'The shuttle station is near the harbour, where you arrived last night.' She opened a drawer and took out a sheet of paper. 'Take this. It's a map of Santa Cruz, and the rest of the island. Be careful on your journey and don't tell too many people why you are here.'

'Which people?'

'Anyone who asks why you are going to Los Gigantes.'

I looked at Calista, and said to the woman. 'Why would anyone want to know why we are going to Los Gigantes?'

Trevor William Poate

'Strangers usually only go there for one reason. I think you know what I mean…freedom.' She looked at me as though she was deciding what to say next.

'Thank you. We will be careful,' I said. I guessed we weren't the first people she had helped.

She took the map from me and wrote a name on the back. 'Ask some people in Los Gigantes' harbour for that name. Say you were sent by me, Maria Xabi.'

I looked at the name she had written. Guanche. 'Thank you. Thank you very much,' I said, taking the map and shaking her hand.

We collected our bags from the room. The long-haired man was still sitting outside the cantina as we left the hotel, and made our way to the shuttle station, glancing behind us every few metres to see if he was following us. He wasn't.

We found the station without any problem and made our way to the ticket office. The man selling the tickets told us the next shuttle to Los Gigantes left half an hour later, so we found some seats on the platform, where we waited for it to arrive, trying to look inconspicuous.

When it arrived, a few minutes early, we made our way along the platform, boarded, and found two seats near the front. It soon filled up with people, busily chatting to each other. Just before it left, the long haired-man also boarded, and sat near us.

The map Maria had given us, showed Los Gigantes to be about a hundred kilometres along the coast, an hour and a half on the shuttle. We would be there before lunchtime, giving us plenty of time to look around and find somewhere to stay. We thought it would take a few days to find out about getting a boat to El Hierro, and knew we would have to be careful who we asked. My main worry was being traced when we used our credits, but there was nothing we could do about that. I hoped Susan was right, that we would have a week before anyone knew where we were.

The long-haired man didn't seem to be taking any notice of us during the first hour of the journey. He just sat and read a newspaper, occasionally looking out of a window.

'If he is following us, I think we should get off at the station before Los Gigantes, and see if he does as well,' I said to Calista. 'Then we'll know.'

'Alright.'

The shuttle stopped soon after, and we got off. He didn't.

'He's stayed on,' I said. 'We'll catch the next one. Let's get a drink while we wait.'

The next shuttle arrived an hour later, and we boarded it, comforted that we weren't being followed. When it arrived in Los Gigantes, we got off with a few other people and looked around the small station.

'He's not here,' I said to Calista.

'Isn't he?' she replied, in a nervous voice. 'Who's that then?'

I looked where she was pointing. The long-haired

man was sitting on a bench outside the station. He glanced at us briefly, than looked back at his newspaper.

We hurriedly left, and found a cantina nearby, sat down, and ordered some food. He hadn't followed us, but we did see him walk past, and glance in our direction, as though confirming where we were. Calista and I looked at each other.

'It's just a coincidence,' I said, unconvinced, but determined to try and put her mind at rest.

'I hope so,' she said, squeezing my hand.

The town was quiet, with only a few people wandering around in the mid-day sun, their wrinkled skin looking like crumpled up paper.

'I wonder where everyone is.' I said, as we ate our food.

'Maybe they're working.'

I looked around the street. 'Maybe,' I said.

'What do we do now?'

I looked at the name on the back of the map. 'Find somewhere to stay, and then ask around for this man, Guanche.'

We finished our lunch and paid the bill. We thought of asking the waiter about somewhere to stay, but decided instead to look around the town and harbour first.

The town was built around a small inlet surrounded by cliffs. On our walk down the hill to the harbour, we passed some closed shops, more cantinas and a few white painted houses, but we didn't see any places to stay, and wondered if we should have asked the waiter.

There were a few fishing boats in the harbour, with one or two men making repairs to nets and other equipment. It reminded me a little of Orzola, but it seemed even more traditional. There were a lot of derelict buildings, which I guessed were left over from when people travelled more than was now possible. The whole place looked to be in decline.

We strolled around the harbour for most of the afternoon, until we eventually found another open cantina. We stopped for a drink and sat at a table outside, on an open terrace. The waiter brought us some tapas and took our order. We hadn't seen the long-haired man again, which helped relax us, as we waited for our drinks.

'We're looking for a room to stay in for a few days,' I said to the waiter, when he came back.

'What sort of room?' he said.

'Just a small room. Do you know of anywhere?'

'I have a room here you can have,' he said. 'Come, I will show you.'

We stood up, followed him through the dark cantina, and up some steps to a room overlooking the terrace. It was small, with a double bed, a place to put our clothes and a walk-in shower.

'How much is it?' I asked.

He looked at me and Calista, and said. 'One hundred credits per night.'

I glanced at Calista who nodded, and said. 'Alright, we'll take it.'

'You can pay me when you leave,' he said.

Trevor William Poate

We followed him back down the stairs to the terrace, finished our drinks, and returned to the room, carrying our bags.

'We should rest for a while and then shower,' I said to her, getting undressed, 'we can unpack later.'

'Perhaps we should ask him if he knows Guanche,' she said, closing the curtains across the window.

'Later. We don't want to make him suspicious.'

'Why should he be suspicious? We only want to find the man.'

'I know, but I think we should be careful for a day or so.'

'Alright, but we don't have very long.'

We spent the evening eating and drinking in the cantina, gauging the feel of the place. It was quite full most of the time, with people I supposed used it regularly. The waiter, Paolo, greeted people as they came and went. Some of them looked at us strangely, glancing in our direction as they whispered to him in Spanish, which we could still only barely understand when spoken quickly. By ten o'clock we'd had enough and went to bed, a little drunk from the local wine. No one except Paolo had spoken to us all evening.

The following morning we woke early, as the sun shone through the thin curtains. Paolo had insisted that everything we ate and drank was added to the bill, so when he offered us breakfast for no charge we were surprised. He sat with us for a while as we ate, and asked us what our plans were. We said we didn't have any, so he suggested we take a walk along the cliffs where he told us there was a beach about two kilometres away, in a small inlet, that we could use for swimming. He also offered to make some lunch to take with us, and suggested we take a bottle of wine. We weren't sure, because we needed to find Guanche.

'Do you know someone called Guanche,' I eventually asked him.

'No I don't,' he said. 'What do you want with him?'

'We were told by someone in Santa Cruz that we might meet him here.'

'I don't know of anyone with that name,' he repeated, 'but I can ask around. Go for your walk. It's a lovely day for swimming.'

I just nodded, and said. 'Yes, I think we will. Thank you for the breakfast.'

He brought us a bag with our lunch and wine, and two towels, gave us directions to the path, and said he'd see us later. I had a feeling he wanted to say something else, but he didn't.

We followed the steep path along the rough black rocks to the top of the cliffs where, looking back, there was a panoramic view of the town. Three fishing boats were returning to the harbour, having made their catch for the day, and there were people bustling around the small market nearby. We walked for about half an hour before we saw a path to our left leading down to the inlet. We could see sand at the bottom, as we carefully descended a set of wooden steps. No one else was there.

We swam a few times, and lay in the warm sun during the morning. A few birds appeared when we started eating our lunch, but they were all we saw until mid afternoon, when we heard someone walking down the steps to the beach. We quickly wrapped the towels around our naked bodies as the man approached us. He was middle aged, looked like a local with his tanned craggy skin, and was obviously fit.

'Good afternoon,' he said, as he started to take off his clothes. 'It's a good day for swimming.'

'Yes,' I said, 'the water is beautiful and clear.'

He laid a towel down near us, folded his clothes as he undressed, and then ran into the water. Once he was in, he waved to us. At first I didn't understand what he meant, but eventually I realised he wanted us to join him in the water.

I looked at Calista and said. 'You wait here. I'll see what he wants.'

'Be careful,' she said, as I stood up and dropped my towel.

'I will.'

I slowly walked to the edge of the water and waded in. He wasn't very far out, and I could stand as I approached him.

'Hello,' I said.

'Hello, he replied. 'My name is David. I'm told

you are looking for Guanche.'

'Yes we are. Who told you?'

'What for?' he said, ignoring my question.

'Someone in Santa Cruz told us to look for him.'

'Who was that?'

'A lady called Maria Xabi. She runs a hotel there.'

'Tell your wife to join us here.'

I turned around and waved at Calista to come and join us. When she arrived I told her the man's name, and said he was asking why we wanted to meet Guanche. She looked at me, unsure what to say, and started shaking, so I went over to her and held her.

'We want to go to El Hierro.' I said to him.

'Why?'

I looked at Calista, uncertain what to tell him. I decided to be brave. 'We were told we would have to go to a Detention Centre, and because we don't want to we came here. Someone told us Renegades live on El Hierro and we might be able to join them.'

'Were you in the European Complex?' he asked, unexpectedly.

'You know about that?' Calista said, holding me more closely.

'Yes, I know about it. Were you there?'

'Yes, we were,' I said.

'What did you do wrong?'

'Nothing. They just said we were being difficult.'

He looked at both of us. I thought he was trying to decide if we were telling the truth.

Trevor William Poate

'If you are lying to me...'

'...we're not,' I said, interrupting him and raising my voice above the noise of the breaking waves. 'We came here to try and live a free life. If you think we are some kind of...spies, you're wrong.'

'You came here from Lanzarote. Who helped you?'

'Yes, we did. How do you know that?'

'Who helped you?' he repeated, emphasising his words.

'A woman called Susan and a man called Pablo. They were unhappy about us being sent to the Detention Centre.'

'Why?'

'Because they knew we hadn't done anything wrong,' I said, raising my voice again.

'You are not the first to try to go to El Hierro. But not everyone is allowed to,' he said, looking at us with a penetrating stare.

'Why not?'

'Some people are not suitable. Why do you think you are?'

'I don't know. We just...well, we can't stay here. We'll eventually be caught, taken back, and put in detention.'

'If I help you, you will have to go soon, probably in two or three days. But other people will want to talk with you first. Once you've been accepted, and go to El Hierro, you won't be able to leave. Do you understand that?'

I looked at Calista, who nodded at me in confirmation. 'Yes, we do. When will we meet Guanche?'

'You'll find out about Guanche later.'

'Did Paolo tell you about us?' Calista said.

'He just confirmed what I'd heard about you from someone in the cantina last night. He also sent you here at my request, so we could talk without anyone overhearing us. Don't question him, he doesn't know anything of importance.'

'Who told you about us?'

'It doesn't matter at the moment.' He looked at us, paused, and turning his head to look at the beach, said. 'I've had my swim. I'll go back now, and be in touch with you again soon. Stay here and enjoy your swim. Don't tell anyone that you've met me, including Paolo, and don't use your credits to buy anything. If everything works out, I'll settle your bill with Paolo.'

'Alright,' I said, as he started wading towards the shore. I thought for a moment, and shouted to him. 'We've already used our credits at a cantina near the shuttle station, the hotel in Santa Cruz and for our tickets here from Santa Cruz.'

He stopped and looked at us. 'No you haven't. I've already dealt with them. You are not here.'

'I also think we might have been followed here.'

'You were.'

'You knew we were coming here?'

'Yes. I was told to look out for you.'

'Who by?'

'A friend on Lanzarote. I can't tell you any more now, I must go.'

We stood in silence, watching him dress and leave the beach. Calista was still shivering, but not with cold.

'I hope he can help us,' she said, nervously.

'I don't think he would have come here if wasn't going to.'

'What should we do?'

'Just as he said. Not tell anyone we've spoken with him, and wait for him to contact us again.'

We left the water and stayed on the beach for another hour. By the time we returned to Paolo's cantina there were already a few people sitting outside drinking wine. Paolo greeted us as we entered the bar.

'How was your day?' he asked.

'The beach and water were lovely,' Calista said. 'We might go back tomorrow.'

'You should stay here tomorrow. There will be a fiesta. Everyone dresses up and dances through the streets. There are many parties, and much fun,' he said.

'What is a fiesta?' I asked.

'It's when the whole town parties, in thanks for our happiness.'

'Thanks to who?'

'Thanks to our ancestors.'

I looked at Calista, and said. 'Alright, we'll stay here.'

'Good. I have some special food for you tonight,

some fish I have been preparing all day, especially for you.'

'For us?'

'Yes. Go and shower, and change. It'll be ready in about two hours.'

'Thank you,' I said, glancing at Calista.

We made our way to the room where we were surprised to find a vase full of fresh flowers, and a note which said, 'I will see you soon'. We assumed it was from David, but it could have been from anyone, even Guanche.

The bar was nearly full when we entered. Paolo showed us to a table and brought us some red wine.

'I will bring your fish very soon,' he said. 'Drink some wine.'

Everyone sitting around us were chatting and smiling, and a few glanced over at us as I poured the wine.

Paolo returned with our food. 'This is Bocinegro, a la sal,' he said, pointing at the fish. 'I baked it especially for you. And this is Papa Arrugadas,' he said, pointing to what appeared to be wrinkled potatoes cooked in their skins. 'The sauce is Red Mojo. It is made with hot peppers and is very spicy. Use it carefully.'

The food looked beautiful. We thanked him and started eating. The fish was soft and tasted quite salty, the insides of the potatoes were light and fluffy and the skins crispy, but the sauce was almost too hot. I managed some, but Calista nearly choked on her first taste. The people at the table next to us heard her, and laughed, in a friendly way.

The atmosphere in the room seemed much friendlier than the previous evening. Two men were playing guitars, and a few women were dancing, seductively. I guessed it was the start of the fiesta.

Paolo kept bringing jugs of wine, and by the time we'd finished eating, and drinking, it was midnight. However, that wasn't the end of the evening. People were still dancing, and before we were allowed to leave Paolo insisted we join in. They were laughing and clapping, giving us encouragement, as we tried to follow their movements! Just before we finally escaped to bed, I noticed David, sitting at the bar. He glanced at me and smiled, then returned to the conversation he was having with the long-haired man. I didn't approach him, thinking he wouldn't want anyone to know we knew him. I just pointed him out to Calista, as we made our way to our room.

'Did you see who David was talking to?' I said, as we undressed for bed.

'Yes. It was the man from the boat and the shuttle.'

'He must have followed us and told David we'd arrived. We should be careful. We don't really know who they are.'

'You don't think they'll send us back, do you?' she said, anxiously.

'I don't know, but we'll soon find out.'

Trevor William Poate

209

Chapter 6

Guanche

*W*e woke late the next morning with sore heads from the evening's drinking. There seemed to be a lot of noise coming from outside. I looked out of the window and saw a parade of brightly dressed people marching down the street. Some were banging drums, some playing guitars, and some just making a lot of noise. They all seemed excited, jumping up and down, singing, and appearing to be sober, which was more than I was.

Paolo must have heard us moving around, because he was waiting for us with what he called his 'cure' when we went down to the bar, hoping for something to fill our stomachs.

'Drink this,' he said, smiling in a manner that suggested he thought our delicate condition was funny.

'What is it?' Calista said.

'Just drink it. You'll feel better. I'll bring you some breakfast, and then you can join in the fun outside.'

I looked at him as though he was a fool. 'I don't think we'll be joining in anything for a while,' I said, very quietly, smiling at Calista who was holding her head in her hands.

'You will. Trust me,' he said, returning my smile.

We drank his 'cure', which tasted horrible, and returned to our room after eating some breakfast. Neither of us felt very well, so we decided to lie down again for a while. It must have been two or three hours before we woke up. David, was sitting on a chair opposite the bed.

'What are you doing here?' I said.

'I want to have a talk with you about El Hierro.'

'Now?' I said, rubbing my eyes, and nudging Calista to wake up.

'Yes. Now. Get ready, and I'll meet you downstairs. Don't be long.'

He left the room as I started to get to my feet. 'We'd better get ready,' I said to Calista, as she started to wake up.

She stood up and said. 'I feel better now. Do you?'

I thought for a moment, and said, 'Yes, I think I do.'

We quickly washed, and went downstairs. David was sitting at the bar with the long-haired man, who he introduced as Andreas. The man nodded, but didn't speak.

'Come with us. There's someone you should meet,' David said.

We followed the two of them out of the bar, through crowds of people singing and dancing, and along the quay to a large, yellow and black painted, fishing boat. The boat was called 'Guanche'.

'We thought Guanche was a person,' Calista said, glancing at me.

Trevor William Poate

211

'The Guanches were the native inhabitants before the Europeans invaded the islands,' David said, as he walked up a short gangway to the deck. 'Mind your step.'

Calista and I went next, closely followed by Andreas. We entered a darkened room below the deck, near the rear of the boat.

'I want you to meet someone,' David said, pausing before switching on a light.

Calista screamed with fright as soon as she saw the person sitting at a small table opposite us. 'What's wrong with her?' she said, shaking at the sight in front of us.

'She's the result of one of the Consortium's experiments in eugenics. She's one of the twins from your Complex,' Andreas said, speaking for the first time.

'How old is she?'

'How old are you?' he said, looking Calista in the eyes.

She stared back at him, and then at the old woman. Her eyes widened, and she suddenly lost all the colour in her cheeks. 'You don't mean…she's my twin?'

I thought she was going to faint, but she just slumped to the floor. David stood near the door, quietly watching.

'Yes, she is. We call her Maria. She's been on El Hierro for nearly fifteen years. If you go there your work will involve looking after people like her,' he said, kneeling down next to her.

I quickly moved over to Calista, knelt down and, putting my arms around her, said to him. 'How many are there on the island?'

'About four thousand twins. They're not all as bad as her. Some are sick, and some are deformed. The other two thousand people on the island are helpers, as you would be.'

'We were told our twins were fostered out, as part of the experiment,' I said.

'Some are, and some are used for medical experimentation. Most of them, the ones used in the experiments, end up on El Hierro or somewhere similar, or dead.'

'Is my twin there?'

'He was, but he died a long time ago.'

'Are you sure she's Calista's twin?'

'Yes, I'm sure. We've checked their DNA. There's no doubt.'

I moved towards the old woman, breaking away from Calista.

'It's alright. You can touch her,' he said. 'She's not infectious, and barely even knows you are here. Since she arrived, like most of them, she has degenerated into her current condition. Her brain and body have become prematurely old over the last few years.'

'What happened to her?' I said.

'The Consortium's experiments are designed to extend the human life span and eradicate disease. She is one of the failures. She looks as though she is seventy or eighty years old, but she's only twenty three, the same as Calista.'

'Why didn't they just...just kill her,' I said, looking at the old woman.

'Even the Consortium has some morals. They don't kill anyone. They just send them to places like El Hierro.'

I stared at the old woman, trying to understand how anyone could be so old, but so young. 'Who told you we were coming here?' I said, looking at David.

'Mary.'

'Mary knew we were coming here?'

'She organised it with Robert.'

'But I thought Susan and Pablo helped us.'

'They did, but they don't know everything.'

'But Mary wanted us to go to the Detention Centre.'

'She realised you could become a problem, so she told you you were being sent to a Detention Centre, in case you spoke with any of the others in your group, particularly Fabio and Tina. She hasn't yet recommended you are put in detention, but she still can. It will depend on what you decide to do. Allowing you to come here was a test of your resolve to become Renegades.'

I looked down at Calista and Maria, and said. 'What choices do we have?'

'You have three choices. You can go to El Hierro and help look after the twins: you can go back to Graciosa and...well, Mary will have to send you to a Detention Centre to avoid getting herself into any trouble, or you can help us close down the Complex, and stop their experiments. I know Mary took a lot of risks to get you here, so I wouldn't want you to choose the option to return to Graciosa, but you can if you want. However, Mary thinks you may be the best chance we've had in years to stop the Consortium.'

I was confused, and Calista was still distraught and staring at her twin. 'How long do we have, to decide?' I asked.

'You have a few days, but the sooner the better,' Andreas said.

'If we decide to help stop the Consortium, how do we do it?'

'Make your decision and we'll make the arrangements.'

'Can you tell us more before we decide?'

'No. I'm sorry but I can't. You need to trust me.'

I looked at Calista's twin, the old woman sitting at the table, totally oblivious to our being there, and said. 'Alright, give us a few days.'

David looked at Andreas, who nodded, and said. 'Alright, I'll be in touch in a few days. Don't talk to Paolo about what you've seen here today.'

'No, we won't.'

'Now, go and enjoy the fiesta, but be back at Paolo's by nine o'clock. Two of your old friends will be there. Talk with them. They may help you make up your minds.'

'Who are they?' I said, glancing at Calista.

'Karl and Monica.'

The shock of seeing Calista's twin spoilt our party mood. Instead of joining in the fiesta we decided to return to Paolo's. We went to our room and lay on the bed, holding each other tightly.

'What should we do?' Calista eventually said.

'We should hear what Karl and Monica have to say before we decide.'

'They must be living on El Hierro.'

'I wonder what they are doing there.'

I looked at my watch. It was nearly eight o'clock.

'Let's go down and have some food. They'll be here soon.'

'I'm not very hungry.'

'Neither am I, but we should eat something.'

We went down to the bar, which was full of people celebrating the fiesta. Paolo found us a table, brought some wine and suggested something to eat. We told him some tapas would do. He frowned, and said we should eat more, but we insisted we didn't want anything else.

I looked around the bar, and the tables outside, but Karl and Monica weren't there, neither were David or Andreas. We sat in silence sipping our wine and listening to the chatter of the people at the adjacent tables.

It was soon after nine o'clock when I saw Karl enter the bar, with Monica a few steps behind him. I stood up and caught their attention. They smiled, came over to our table, and gave us both a long hug. I noticed she had put on weight. Paolo came over to us, found two chairs for them, and brought us some more wine and tapas.

'When did you get here?' Karl asked us, after they had sat down.

'Three days ago,' I said.

'Andreas has asked us to tell you about the island. What do you want to know?'

'Everything. What the twins are like: the helpers, how you live, everything.'

Karl looked at Monica and said. 'Where do we start?'

'Tell them about what we do,' Monica said.

'What has Andreas told you?' Karl asked.

'Only that there are about four thousand twins, and two thousand helpers, and that the twins are mostly sick or deformed in some way, as a result of the Consortium's experimentation.'

'Not all of them are twins. There are a few hundred people who have been sent there because they caused trouble in the Complex, and were dealt with.'

'What do you mean, 'dealt with'.'

'They have had surgery to remove their memories of the Complex.'

'Brain surgery?' Calista said, loudly.

'Yes.'

'How did you get here? You haven't had surgery.'

'The same way as you did. Mary also helped us escape, but the Officers are beginning to lose trust in her, and Robert. You may be the last.'

'Did you meet Maria?' Monica said, changing the

subject, and looking around to see if anyone had heard Calista.

'Yes. This afternoon.'

'Then you know she's your twin.'

I looked at Calista, and said. 'Yes, we do.'

'She's a rarity. Most of the twins have some physical deformity, usually internal, such as malfunctioning organs. Quite a few have had brain surgery, which has left them passive, or...retarded, and others have shortened limbs or missing fingers and toes. The only thing they have in common is that they can't look after themselves.'

'How many do you look after?' Calista asked.

'We work in groups of ten looking after twenty or thirty at a time, depending on what's wrong with them.'

'How old are they?'

'They range from about ten to fifty or more. Not many live to that age though.'

'What about food and water?'

'Some of the helpers farm the land, and others work the wind farm and fresh water systems. We also have a small hospital, which we get some supplies for from here. Other medicines we make from plants and minerals found on the island,' Karl said.

'Are you totally self sufficient?' I said.

'Apart from some of the medicines, and the occasional spare parts for the wind farm, yes we are.'

'Do you like it there?'

'Like it? I suppose we do. We've only been there

three months, but, yes I think we do,' Karl said, looking at Monica.

'There's a sort of satisfaction in helping people,' she said, looking at Calista, 'but you have to be prepared to work hard.'

'Who's in charge?'

'It doesn't work like that. Everyone has an opportunity to say what they feel. There is a committee which everyone takes turns on, so no one is in charge.'

'Do you think we should go there?' Calista said.

'You have to decide that. What options have they given you?'

'Joining you; returning to Graciosa and going into detention, or helping to stop the Consortium's experiments.'

'There are no Detention Centres…it's a euphemism for El Hierro and other places like it. Have you been told how you would help stop them?'

'No. Not yet.'

'I know Andreas and David are looking for people to return to the Complex as trainers, in the Quarantine Centre.'

'How will that help stop the Consortium?' I said.

'They want some people to free everyone in the Complex, and prove that it's safe outside.'

'How?'

'I don't know the details, just that they need someone with computer skills.'

'Why don't we just tell everyone outside what is

happening in the Complexes?' Calista said.

'How? The Federal Government controls all the public information announcements, and the newspapers.'

'But we could just tell people.'

'That's been tried. The people spreading the stories ended up on El Hierro, and everyone else is frightened.'

'They were operated on?' I said.

'Yes.'

'If the Federal Government knows about all of you, why do they let you stay on the island?'

'They need us as helpers, but not many of us are escapees, most have been operated on. They appear normal, but don't remember where they were before.'

Paolo brought us some more wine and tapas, and sat down at our table. 'You should be careful what you say. People are listening,' he said, quietly.

I looked around. Nobody seemed to be watching us, or taking any notice of what we were saying.

'Are you sure?' I said.

He stood up and said. 'Yes, I am.'

We lowered our voices and talked for another hour before Karl stood up and said. 'We should go.'

'Already?' Calista said.

'Yes. We are going back tonight.'

'How?'

'On the Guanche.'

'I hope we've helped you decide,' Monica said, looking around the bar.

'Yes, I think you have. One other question. Were

you asked to go back?'

Karl looked at Monica, and said. 'Yes, we were, but Monica is pregnant, so we couldn't.' He shook his head and, continuing, said. 'Otherwise we would have gone. It's important you do this, for everyone.'

We hugged each other, and they left, just as David came in and made his way to the bar. He didn't look at us, until we stood up to go back to our room a little while later. He spoke with Paolo, who came over and said we should stay, and enjoy the music and dancing.

We didn't see David the next day. We went to the beach where there were a few people recovering from the festivities, and ate at Paolo's that evening.

The following day the beach was empty. We lay on the sand and swam a little until lunchtime, when David arrived.

'Have you decided?' he said.

'Where were you yesterday?' I said.

'I took Karl: Monica, Maria, and Andreas, back to El Hierro on the Guanche.'

'I thought Andreas was taking them back.'

'No. Andreas lives there, and the Guanche would be missed if it didn't return here.'

'I want to go to El Hierro before I decide,' Calista said to him.

'There isn't time for that. We want you to go back to the Complex, as trainers in the Quarantine Centre, but you need to leave soon, otherwise you will be missed.

Mary and Robert have hidden your absence so far, but they can't for much longer. Also, Patricia and Ronaldo are leaving the Complex next week and going to work in the Rehabilitation Centre, replacing Susan and Pablo who are going away for a while. You could take over from them in the Complex after they leave.'

'If we go back and tell everyone it's safe outside, what will happen to them?' I said.

'They will leave, and be free.'

'And what will happen to the Flora Centre and the Fauna Centre?'

'They can continue. It's only the eugenics experiments we want to see stopped.'

'Why us. Why not Mary and Robert?'

'Karl told you what we want you to do?'

'Yes, he did.'

'Mary and Robert have never been inside the main Complex, that's why we need you to go there.'

'But how can we help you if we are in the Quarantine Centre?'

'You'll have access to the rest of the Complex as well.'

'So Mary is really on our side,' Calista said.

'Yes, but she has to be careful. As I told you, allowing you to come here was a test of your resolve to become Renegades. She also wanted my opinion of you. She told the Federal Government you were being given extra training. If you go back, she will either make sure you go to the Quarantine Centre as trainers, to replace

Patricia and Ronaldo or, as I've already told you, she will have to send you to a Detention Centre to avoid getting into trouble herself. If you decide not to go back she, and Robert, may …well they may end up on El Hierro. The Officers are becoming suspicious.'

'What did she tell Fabio and Tina?'

'She told them you were going to be assessed further, before a final decision was made to send you to a Detention Centre, or elsewhere.'

'Won't they be suspicious if we turn up at the Quarantine Centre as trainers?'

'That's a risk we'll have to take.'

'You mean, 'we'll have to take'.'

'Yes.'

'When must we decide?' I said.

'Before tomorrow. If you agree to go, you'll need to leave on the early morning shuttle,' he said, standing up to leave. 'I'll see you at Paolo's tonight. You can tell me your decision then.'

'If we do as you ask and get caught, what will happen to us?' Calista said.

He went quiet for a moment. 'You'll probably end up on El Hierro, but not as helpers.'

The Dancing Dolls

Trevor William Poate

Part Three

Release

Trevor William Poate

The Dancing Dolls

Trevor William Poate

Chapter 1

The Quarantine Centre

*P*atricia and Ronaldo met us when we arrived at the Quarantine Centre. They were staying for an extra week to help us learn more about our new work, and show us around, before transferring to the Rehabilitation Centre.

'I never thought we'd see you again,' Patricia said, smiling at us as we left the shuttle.

'We never expected to return here,' I said, as I shook Ronaldo's hand.

'We were surprised when Mary and Robert told us you had been chosen to join the retraining group,' Ronaldo said.

'So were we.'

Patricia looked at Ronaldo, and said. 'We'll show you to your accommodation. When you've unpacked we thought you might like to join us for dinner in our accommodation, and then you can tell us about why you decided to join us.'

'Alright,' I replied, glancing at Calista who had been unusually quiet up to that point.

'Where is your accommodation?' she asked.

'Next to yours.'

We joined them a couple of hours later. They had cooked a pleasant meal, and we even had a bottle of wine. They asked us some general questions about our time outside, and the Rehabilitation Centre. They were looking forward to returning there for the first time in four months. Eventually the conversation turned to why we were there.

'Why did you decide to become trainers?' Patricia asked.

Calista looked at me, and said to her. 'Are we being overheard?'

'Not in here.'

'What have Mary and Robert told you about us?'

'Only that you were chosen to join our group.'

'They didn't tell you why?'

Patricia looked at Ronaldo, who nodded at her. 'We know them very well. We also agree with a lot of their ideas about…'

'What ideas?' I said, interrupting her.

'Their ideas…about the Complex.'

'Tell us about their…ideas.'

She looked at Ronaldo again, and said. 'Let me explain who we are. Ronaldo and I are products of the Complex. We are both second twins. Our other twins are still in the Complex. Mary and Robert, and Susan and Pablo are the same. We were lucky not to have been used by the Consortium for experiments. Instead we were fostered by families outside, and groomed for our work here. Because our twins are still inside the Complex, we are not allowed to go there. You are, and that's why Mary and Robert recommended you for our group.'

'But why us, there must have been other people before?' Calista said.

'You both showed determination not to conform, and you, Callum, have the technical knowledge we need. Also, Calista, we know you've seen your twin, and know the outcome of some of the experiments. We know you were shocked by what you saw, and what Karl and Monica told you.'

'You know we saw them?'

'Yes. We know everything you did while you were away from here.'

'But surely there must have been other people Mary could have chosen.'

'There were a few, but none of them were prepared to come back here.'

'Surely the Officers had to be consulted about appointing us,' I said.

'They were, but they trust Mary and Robert's opinions, at the moment.'

'What about Fabio and Tina? Were they asked about us?'

Ronaldo looked at Patricia, paused, and said. 'They won't be a problem.'

'Why not?'

'They had an accident. They're not here.'

'What sort of accident?'

'They didn't make it here, from Graciosa I mean.'

'What happened?'

''There was an 'accident' on the boat. They slipped and fell overboard.'

'But Robert and Mary and…and David, think they are here.'

'We haven't told them yet. They'll know soon.'

'And what about your opinions? Do the Officers believe you?'

'Yes. They trust us as well.'

'Can we trust you?'

'You have to, if you want to help.'

There was a pause as Calista and I looked at each other, silently making up our minds.

'You'd better tell us what you want us to do,' I eventually said.

Patricia looked at Ronaldo, and said. 'Ronaldo will tell you the plan…'

It had been a late night discussing Ronaldo's plan. Afterwards, in our own accommodation, we discussed what had happened to Fabio and Tina. We both thought it unlikely that they had both had an accident, and were concerned about how far Robert and Mary would go to protect themselves. We slept fitfully, worrying about it. The next morning we returned to Patricia and Ronaldo's accommodation for breakfast. We didn't have any food of our own, but would be given some later that day.

We knew the Officers would be monitoring our progress for the first few days, when we were being shown around the Centre, and being told all we needed to know about the training. We met a few of the Officers who ran the Centre, were shown areas we hadn't seen when we were being retrained and, most importantly, I was given the access codes for the computer systems. I was allowed to spend time learning them and, crucially, I found out what I needed to know for the plan to work.

We only spoke about the plan in Patricia and Ronaldo's accommodation during the evenings, fine-tuning what we were going to do. They were due to leave at the end of the week, and we needed to implement it before they left. We were lucky there were no people being retrained at the time, and none were expected for at least two more weeks. Unless the Officers made some unscheduled expulsions, we were only expecting some retirees. Ronaldo told us none of the second twins ever went to the Quarantine Centre or the Rehabilitation Centre. They were transported, directly from the Eugenics Centre, to El Hierro.

Our main problem was finding a reason to visit the Centre. Once there, we thought we could put the plan into action very easily, but time was running out if Patricia and Ronaldo were to help us. Otherwise, we would have to wait until Susan and Pablo arrived a week later.

Our opportunity arrived unexpectedly, three days before they were due to leave.

Chapter 2

Relief

*O*ne of the Officers came to our accommodation while we were eating, on our fourth evening, and told us we were being sent to the Centre the next morning.

'Why?' I asked.

'We want you to help out with the relief group for a few days. We are short of people with your skills. Ronaldo and Patricia will stay here for another week to finish off your training when you return.'

I looked at Calista, and said. 'But you must have plenty of people who can do relief work.' I was trying my best to sound disappointed at the transfer, when I was really elated. I knew it was our chance, and I also knew it was going to be dangerous. I didn't really want Calista to be put at risk, and had told her, Patricia, and Ronaldo that I could make the plan work by myself. They had argued that the Officers rarely split couples up. It was both of us, or neither of us.

'Alright. When do we go?'

'Be ready at six o'clock tomorrow morning. A security man will come for you.'

'How long will we be there?' Calista asked.

'A week.'

'Where will we be going?'

'One of the Multiplexes.'

The officer gave us a strange smile, and said. 'You won't need to take anything with you. We'll provide it all.'

I looked at him and said, 'Nothing?'

'That's right, nothing. I'll go now.'

'Do you think they know about the plan?' Calista said, in a whisper, after he'd left us.

'I hope not. We should go and tell Patricia and Ronaldo.'

We quickly finished our meal and went to their accommodation.

'We're being sent to the Centre tomorrow, to help with the relief group for a week,' I told them. 'The Officer was strange. He said we didn't need to take anything.'

'Really? You'll need to take your workbook, it has all the access codes,' Ronaldo said.

'I know. I'll take it anyway. I'll think up some reason why I need it.'

'Can you do what you need to from one of the Multiplexes?' Patricia asked.

'Yes, I think so.'

'Good. Do it on Friday, the last day before we leave. We'll look after things at this end.'

'The officer told us you will be staying another week, until after we return.'

Patricia looked at Ronaldo and said. They haven't

told us that.'

'They told us.'

'Alright.'

We spent an hour going through the plan again, before leaving and getting ready for the next morning. Patricia seemed nervous the whole time we talked, constantly looking at Ronaldo, and saying very little herself. I wondered if she was worried about meeting her twin, or what would happen to them if we were caught.

'It'll be strange eating the paste again,' Calista said, as we lay in bed.

'If everything works out, it won't be for long.'

'I hope so.'

The security man came for us at six o'clock. Initially he didn't want me to take my workbook, but relented when I told him I would need it to work the systems. The Officer we'd seen the previous evening was at the shuttle waiting for us. He also wanted me to leave my workbook, but when I refused he relented, reluctantly.

We sat silently for most of the two hour journey, not wanting to say anything to make the security man accompanying us suspicious. We were surprised when Johannes met us, and took us to an Officer's consulting room. Something didn't seem right.

The Officer behind the desk told us to sit down.

'Callum, Calista, it's good to see you again.'

'Have we met?' I said.

'Yes. I was with Johannes when you said you

didn't want to be reassigned.'

I thought for a moment, and said. 'Oh yes, I remember now.'

'We've brought you here to help us.'

'I thought you needed us to do some relief work,' Calista said.

'We do. But first I have a few questions for you. Tell me about your plan.'

Calista looked at me. She'd visibly turned white.

'What plan?' I said, trying to remain composed.

'The plan you've been talking about in your accommodation at the Quarantine Centre.'

'Have you been listening to us?'

'We listen to everyone. So, tell me about your plan.'

'I don't know what you mean.'

'That's disappointing. We've spent a lot of time and effort on you both, and given you chances most people don't have. So, just tell me about it.' He was doing his best to be persuasive, and pleasant.

I knew we hadn't said anything about the details of the plan in our accommodation, only in Patricia and Ronaldo's, and they had told us we were not being overheard.

'The only plan we have is to do our work, and start a family,' I said. 'There is no other plan.'

He looked at Johannes, who came over to us and said. 'Tell us about your time in the Rehabilitation Centre.'

'What about it?'

'Tell us what you did there.'

'We did what we were told. We learnt about shopping, clothes, and spent time training for our new work.'

'What else did you do?'

I thought for a moment. 'We went to a cantina a few times, and swam. What else should we have done?'

'What did you do in your fifth week?'

I looked at Calista and said. 'While we were waiting to hear if we were going to the Quarantine Centre as trainers, we did some more training.'

'Who was that with?'

'Mary and Robert.'

'Is that all you did?'

'Yes, I think so.'

'You didn't go to Tenerife?'

'Tenerife? Where's that?' I said, trying to sound surprised.

Johannes ignored my question, and said. 'So you didn't meet any Renegades while you were there?'

'Renegades? As far as I know there aren't any on Graciosa.'

'And you Calista. Did you meet any?'

'No, I don't think so,' she said, glancing at me.

'You showed a lot of interest in them while you were there. Why was that?'

'Who told you that?' I said, my voice rising.

'We talk to many people.'

Trevor William Poate

I looked at Calista, and said. 'We just asked a few questions. Nothing very much.'

'And you didn't meet Maria?'

'Who's Maria?' I said, trying to sound confused.

They went quiet for a moment before Johannes said. 'Wait here for a few minutes please.'

'Yes of course,' I said.

They both left the room. I put my fingers up to my lips to tell Calista to be quiet. I guessed we were being listened to.

Johannes returned on his own, about ten minutes later. 'Come with me,' he said.

'Where are we going?' I asked.

'To talk with Fabio and Tina.'

Calista and I looked at each other. 'Where are they?' I said.

'Follow me.'

We left the room and walked down the corridor to another room where Fabio and Tina were sitting behind a table.

'Hello,' Fabio said as we entered, 'how are you?'

'We're fine. We were told you'd had an accident, and were dead.'

'No. We didn't, although...some people think we did.'

'What have you been saying about us?' I said.

'Only what we know.'

'And what is that?'

'We know you were showing an unusual interest in

the Renegades, and we'd like to know why.'

'We have no interest in the Renegades, other than curiosity,' Calista said, in a shaky voice.

'You've asked a lot of questions about them, both here and on Graciosa. There must be a better reason than curiosity.'

'There isn't.'

'Can we trust you not to talk to anyone about the outside?' Tina said.

'Of course you can. We know we can't talk about it to anyone here,' I said.

'Johannes,' Fabio said, 'I still think they need looking after, and then sending to El Hierro.'

'El Hierro?' Calista screamed.

'So, you've heard of it?' Tina said, smiling in a way that suggested we'd been caught saying something we shouldn't have.

'We heard about it in Arrecife, from our trainers,' I said, hurriedly trying to cover up Calista's indiscretion.

'Why would they tell you about it?'

'They mentioned it one day, when we were talking about the other islands.'

'What did they tell you?'

'Nothing really. Just that there is an island called El Hierro where we are not allowed to go.'

'Did they tell you why?'

'No, I don't think so.'

'Their reports tell us you asked them about the Renegades.'

Trevor William Poate

'They must have been mistaken.'

'Is that right? Johannes, I think we should talk, privately,' Fabio said, in a voice that sounded menacing. 'Take them back to the other room.'

We'd only been there a few minutes, and it seemed like we'd been accused, tried and convicted. He took us back to the first room we'd been in, and told us to wait. An hour later he returned and told us we would leave later that afternoon.

'Where are we going?' I asked.

'To the Multiplex where you will be doing your relief work.' He paused for a moment. 'Before we go, remember, you don't talk to anyone about the outside. We'll decide your future while you are away.'

'No. We won't talk to anyone, but…what will you do with us?'

'You'll find out when you return here, next week.'

Trevor William Poate

Chapter 3

The Plan

*W*e arrived at the Multiplex early in the afternoon. It was exactly the same as the one we had lived in. Everything we needed was waiting for us. All our toiletry needs, clean clothes and bedding. Our food packs were also there. I guessed the nutritionists still had our details on the computer records, and had used them to produce the packs.

'It's like we've gone back in time,' Calista said, as we looked around.

'I should check the systems,' I said.

'You do that, while I get some food ready. I'm starving.'

I made my way to the computer room, and switched them on. To be safe, I first checked the systems we needed to work with, before moving on to the systems I needed to complete the plan. After an hour, I went to the feeding room and told Calista everything was alright. I had access to the programs I needed. I'd expected to have had my access rescinded, but they obviously didn't think I was a threat, and had no idea what I was going to do.

'Do you think it's safe to talk in here,' she said, in a whisper.

'As long as we only talk about our work, and general things,' I replied, also in a whisper.

'Let's eat,' she said, moving towards me and giving me an embrace. 'Will everything be alright?' she said.

'Yes, I think so. We'll do our normal work tomorrow, and then in the evening I'll set things up for Friday.' I was still whispering.

'We'd better eat.'

'Yes. Ok.'

Our work the following day went uneventfully. We collected the readings from the Observation room, water, air, and electricity equipment, and I sent them to the Centre. The systems worked as they should, and Calista's lessons weren't a problem.

At the end of our work period, late in the afternoon, we ate our meal and I started getting ready. I didn't have much preparatory work to do, but I couldn't access the computer systems until after midnight because it would have been noticed, when the systems were checked. Every user was monitored at the end of the day, so I needed to make sure I didn't access anything I wasn't expected to, until the start of the day's cycle, at one minute past midnight.

The evening seemed to go on forever. We used our workbooks for reading for a while, but neither of us could concentrate. Instead we just lay in each other's arms on the bed, waiting.

We made our way to the computer room just after midnight and I logged onto the computer systems. I spent an hour setting everything up, and sent a message to Patricia and Ronaldo, telling them everything was ready for six thirty in the morning.

We returned to our bedroom and tried, unsuccessfully, to sleep. If everything worked according to the plan we'd be alright, but if it didn't…El Hierro beckoned, with all it's consequences.

We went to the Observation room at six o'clock as usual, and waited, looking out of the windows at the sand. Our nerves were on edge as the time slipped away. Just before six thirty, Calista came up to me, and held me tightly.

At exactly six thirty, every outside door, in every Observation room, in every Multiplex, made a 'click' and swung open, and the computer monitor alongside each one, sprung to life and announced:

YOU ARE FREE TO LEAVE.
IT IS SAFE OUTSIDE

The warning sounded almost immediately. There was nothing else we could do…

Trevor William Poate

242

DANGER: CONTAMINATION: DANGER:

RETURN TO YOUR MULTIPLEX:

DANGER: CONTAMINATION: DANGER:

RETURN TO YOUR MULTIPLEX:

DANGER…

It kept repeating, and repeating, and repeating…

Chapter 4

A Reality Check

*J*ohn, and his assistant, woke us up late on Sunday afternoon, and took us to another room where Patricia and Ronny were waiting for us.

'Would you like a cup of tea?' Patricia said, as we sat down on two easy chairs.

'Yes please,' we both said.

She went to a side table, poured the tea for us, and brought it over to where we were sitting.

'Before you go we'd like to ask you a few questions about The Experience,' she said, as she sat down opposite to us.

'Alright,' Calista said. She looked pale.

'Before I start, can you both tell me if you enjoyed it?'

I looked at Calista, and said. 'I think so. It was far more realistic than I expected.'

'And you, Calista?'

'It was like I was living it. I was scared a few times.'

'Is that good?'

'I think so. But I'll need a while to come back to

reality.'

'That's not uncommon. Tell me, did you recognise everyone?'

Calista looked at me and said. 'It's hard to tell. While it was happening, I don't think I did, but now I can remember everyone we know that was in it. It's strange how they all fitted in.'

'And you, Callum?'

'The same, I think. Tell me, were their characters based on our experiences of them?'

'Basically yes. They all come from your memories. We link the two of you together with the head scanners, so you can share your thoughts and memories.'

'It's interesting that John, Johannes, and his assistant were the only really bad people. Nearly everyone else helped us.'

John was sitting alongside me, and smiled at my comment. 'If you think about it, your friends are just that: friends. If there had been people who you don't like in your memories, they would probably have been bad people,' he said. 'Also, we usually introduce someone into the story to act as, shall we say, a catalyst for trouble. It makes the whole experience more interesting. That's where I came in.'

'Yes, I suppose so. But, it's interesting that we didn't always trust some of our friends or colleagues, in their characters I mean. I'm thinking of Mary and Robert, my managers at work.'

'My managers are Susan and Peter, or Pablo in the

story,' Calista said.

'You probably don't totally trust them in real life. Employers often don't tell you everything, just what they want you to know.'

I looked at Calista, and said. 'No, I suppose there are one or two things we don't always get to know, when we think we should.'

'Can I have some more tea?' Calista said.

'Yes, of course,' Patricia replied. She picked up our cups, refreshed them, and brought them back.

'Was there anything you didn't like?'

'I didn't like seeing my sister Margaret, or Maria in the story,' Calista said.

'Is your sister ill?'

'She has Hutchinson-Gilford Syndrome, a form of Progeria.'

'I see. That explains why she was depicted as an old person. Do you feel guilty about her condition?'

'I don't know. I know it has nothing to do with me, but I suppose I do feel guilty that I'm alright, and she isn't.'

'Does your sister live at home?'

'No. She's been in care since my parents died, three years ago. Her main carers are called Colin and Martina, or Karl and Monica in the story, and the home is managed by David. That part worked very well. I mean their characters fitted in with reality.'

'Who is Andreas?'

'He's the doctor who looks after Margaret. His real

name is Andrew. It's strange that some people's names changed, and some didn't.'

'It varies with each person. The names sometimes change to nearer what you think the person should be called in The Experience, particularly if it takes place in a foreign country,' Ronny said. 'For example, I was called Ronaldo in the story.'

'What about your pregnancy?' Patricia said.

It was a touchy subject with Calista, and I waited to see her reaction to the question. Eventually, looking at me, she said. 'I, we, lost a baby last year. We are still trying for another one.'

I leant over and held her hand.

'I'm sorry,' Patricia said, clearly realising the delicacy of the subject. 'I'm sure you'll get pregnant again soon.'

'I hope so.'

There was an uncomfortable silence.

'Who are the other people?' John said.

I thought for a few moments. 'Bertrum and Sally are our next door neighbours. The people in the group, Fabio, Kevin, Abigail, and the others, are people we know from our local pub. Fabio is really Fred, a local policeman, so I suppose that fits. He was monitoring us with Christina, his wife. I can't think who the others are.'

'Neither can I,' Calista said, looking at me.

'What about the islands. Were they realistic?'

'Yes. We've been there on holiday a few times, and know all the places,' I said.

'Alright. Is there anything you'd like to ask us?' Ronny said.

I looked at Calista, thought for a moment, and said. 'How much of the story was influenced by us?'

'We just provide the setting for the Complex, and the theme of the story. Everything else is from your imagination.'

'What about the historical stuff?'

'Again, we just provide the outline of possible events. The system has many different options, but it chooses the outline that most closely fits what you already know. For example, you told us at the introduction that you are interested in the effects of global warming, so the system selected a scenario that fitted in with that interest. It could have been another scenario such as a major volcanic eruption, or a virus, which caused The Collapse.'

'What other stories do you have?' Calista asked.

'There are a few. An air crash: a world cruise, a kidnapping, an expedition in Africa or South America, and... others,' she said, shrugging her shoulders. 'You were given 'The Future' for your prize.'

We had won the weekend at the Reality Experience Centre in a competition, and had been given no choice for the theme we would get. The competition involved writing a short story about the future.

'Are they all based on disasters?' I said.

'They are simply themes. They only become a disaster if you turn them into one.'

'How long do they usually last. I mean, ours

covered a period of three or four months in our minds, but in reality it all happened during one weekend here.'

'It varies. Some take place over a few days, and some over months, like yours. It all depends on how the story unfolds.'

'There was nothing really futuristic in the story. Why was that?'

'It comes down to your imagination. The shuttles are based on fact. There are linear powered trains used around the world, and you work with computers so know about them. But unless you are particularly knowledgeable in possible future technologies the story will only reflect what is happening now. Who knows how computer technology will develop, or what medical advances will be made. We may even colonise the Moon, or elsewhere. Perhaps there is life on Mars!'

'Do you think the future will be like that in our story?'

'In my opinion, if people keep fighting, we'll eventually destroy ourselves. We have to stop countries developing nuclear weapons, and other weapons of mass destruction. In any case, I do think we will become more controlled, more restricted and, who knows, more designed. I think that may be the only way congenital diseases will be bred out of us and the human race will survive. It won't be the survival of the fittest; it will be the survival of those fitted for purpose. But, I also think there will be dissidents, rather like the Renegades in your Experience.'

Trevor William Poate

'Heaven help us,' Calista said, looking at me.

'Yes, Heaven. Unfortunately I think religion may be the motivation behind what will destroy the human race,' Patricia said.

'Did you monitor the whole story?' I said.

'Yes. And here's a copy on disc for you to take home,' Ronny said, handing me a DVD.

'I'm not sure I want to go through it again,' Calista said.

'Neither am I,' I said, looking at the disc.

John looked at Patricia, and said. 'Alright, if that's all, you can go. It's been good meeting you. I hope you've enjoyed The Experience.'

'I'm not sure, but I think we did,' I said.

'Good.'

We left, unsure of our feelings.

'I don't think I want to do that again,' I said to Calista, as we made our way home.

'Neither am I. Let's go for a drink, it'll calm my nerves.'

'Alright.'

The pub was nearly full when we entered it. Paul, or Paolo, was behind the bar serving. Abigail and Liam, Kevin and Julia, and Christina and Fred, were sitting together at a table near one of the windows at the front of the room. We bought our drinks, and went over and joined them. I noticed a poster on the wall advertising a 'Spanish' night, with Flamenco Dancing, Cervesa, Spanish wine, and Tapas. I smiled.

'Where have you been?' Kevin asked, as we sat down. 'We haven't seen you all weekend.'

Calista looked at me, and said. 'We spent the weekend at the Reality Experience Centre.'

'Really? Tell us all about it…'

The Dancing Dolls

Trevor William Poate

About the Author

I was born in London in 1955 and moved to Eastbourne in 1968. After leaving school, I trained as an accountant and spent much of the next twenty five years living and working in Africa, the Middle East, North America and Europe.
I started writing in 2008 after spending two years in Ethiopia as a volunteer worker.

www.trevorpoate.co.uk

Other Books by the same author

'Today the Garden Blooms' tells the story of Robert, Mary, and her reluctant lover.
She was single minded and usually got what she wanted, whatever the cost.
Her marriage to Robert was falling apart by the time they went to Zambia. It was a last attempt at saviour, one that would lead to cheating and lies, and eventually tragedy...

Trevor William Poate

253

Rialdo Kane Investigates...

The First Rialdo Kane Investigates...The Key to Dying

When a series of insurance claims relating to household burglaries attracts the attention of Sundown Insurance, Rialdo Kane is asked to investigate. Working undercover, he gains the confidence of Jane Goodall, the attractive daughter of the insurance agent who sold the policies, but his investigation uncovers an unexpected motive for the crimes...

The Second Rialdo Kane Investigates...Accrediting the Dead

After the collapse of Consort Travel, soon after the company received a million pounds in life assurance on the death of two of the directors in a plane crash, Rialdo Kane is asked to investigate the circumstances. His investigation discovers a web of deceit, and that some people are not what they seem...

Trevor William Poate

The Third Rialdo Kane Investigates…A Burning Hatred

Rialdo Kane is asked to investigate when International Insurance suspects arson after a classic car showroom has burnt to the ground. He discovers some of the cars had dubious provenance, and his investigation uncovers a trail of fraud, but the motive doesn't match the crime, until the true culprit explains…

The Fourth Riado Kane Investigates…When Fidelity is Lost

When the accountant at Saxony Clothing is accused of embezzling a quarter of a million pounds, Brightling Insurance asks Rialdo Kane to investigate. He discovers there is a link between Saxony's claim and a series of other claims. Entangled relationships lead him to the conclusion that money wasn't the motive…or was it?

Lightning Source UK Ltd.
Milton Keynes UK
UKOW032015300512

193643UK00016B/112/P